The Defiant Lady

Published [illegible] words

5th Edition

*****

Also by Samantha Garman:

Secrets of a Heart
Charleston Heat
Dandelion Dreams

Chapter I

Hampshire, England, February of 1815

The Dowager Duchess of Cavehill sat on a white chintz settee in the pink drawing room drinking her morning cup of tea, as a fire blazed in the ornate marble hearth dispelling winter's chill. Firelight made the room warm and inviting, and it reminded her how much she loved her country home. Still, she longed for spring, when the gardens would be in bloom, and she could walk among the fragrant white and red rose bushes. The manor was extravagant and lavish, and even though she had not entertained in years, the gold-leafed ballroom could easily hold five hundred guests. The house was too large for just one person, but she never considered a smaller residence. Her home was three stories high, and a hodge-podge of architectural styles. Each successive Duke of Cavehill had made changes that were relevant in their time, and so the Duchess was left with an exceedingly interesting manor that showed the prestige and age of her title.

She smoothed a non-existent crease in her gray dress, a color that signified she was still in mourning. Shut away for nearly a year after the death of her son, Edward, she had not felt the desire to entertain or socialize in months.

She admitted to being lonely, yet the idea of idle conversation over dinner with old friends was unappealing. Perhaps it was time for a companion, someone to sit and read to her. *I am not old enough for a companion*, she thought derisively. She was still young, just past sixty with an upright carriage and a nearly unlined face. Though her hair was mostly gray, her clear, brown eyes sparkled with intellect.

There was a sharp knock on the door, startling the Duchess from her reverie. "Come in," she called. The Duchess's aging butler stepped into the room and handed her a letter.

"This just came for you, Your Grace," Benson spoke.

"Thank you. I will have another cup of Twinings." She quickly dismissed him and examined the nondescript, white envelope. It had come from Paris, and though she had many friends there, she did not recognize the return address, or the handwriting. Perhaps someone was writing with news of Napoleon and his dastardly war.

Opening the letter, she scanned it quickly and then let it fall to her lap. She sat in silence awhile and gazed out the window. Swirling snow drifted down from the white sky and covered the bare trees, and even after Benson brought her another cup of tea, she did not move. She was lost in thought regarding the letter's contents.

Cursing the dead would be in bad taste, but she could not stem her angry thoughts. Her son was deceased, yet his indiscretions remained. Edward had done his duty as any good son would, and at five and twenty, had married a woman of quality. He subsequently produced an heir who ensured proper succession of the dukedom. And, like other men of the gentry, Edward kept a mistress discreetly tucked away—a Parisian ballet dancer who had given him two daughters.

Two daughters the Duchess had known nothing about until Benson handed her a letter that irrevocably changed her life.

The note was from the eldest girl, Ivy Sinclair.

Ivy's letter dripped with desperation, beseeching the Duchess's aid to save them from the misery of peasant life. The older woman was still reeling from the scandalous news, even as she contemplated what to do. She was at the pinnacle of society, and had more to lose, farther to fall with such disgrace.

Damn Edward for leaving me such a mess. It was good fortune her grandson, Robert, was away touring the Continent. She could only imagine his outrage to learn of his father's indiscretions and that he had two half sisters. She contemplated sending him a letter apprising him of the situation, but there had been no word from him for months and she had no clue as to his current location. Robert's communication had been non-existent since the death of his father. The Duchess simply awoke one morning to find Robert gone, with no hint as to his plans for return. At least he had left a note stating his desire to see the continent, and not done something asinine like join in the war against Napoleon.

The Duchess had lost her husband five years prior; she had married for love, though it was good fortune that William had been a duke. Their only child and heir had died and now, her grandson was gallivanting on a war stricken continent.

She was alone, and she had never been so lonely.

How could my son have two children out of wedlock without providing for them financially? The Duchess thought acerbically. His mistakes were not only glaring her in the face, but it was her duty to attend to them. If she sent for them, all of London would know her shame, yet she could not turn her back on their plight. They were family, after all. Perhaps there was a way to minimize the damage.

The Duchess would not yield to the baser instincts of her displeasure, as was her right. Recently, her physician had told her to be mindful of her temper. It was not good for her heart. She wished she were fifteen years younger so she could rant as she pleased.

She closed her eyes all of a sudden feeling very weary. She had asked Benson for a second cup of tea, but she should have demanded a tall glass of sherry instead.

***

Le Havre, France

"What do you think the Duchess of Cavehill is like?" Willow asked curiously. She pulled the collar of her thin, light-blue coat against her neck in hopes of blocking the sea wind.

Ivy shrugged and huddled closer to her younger, taller sister. "Probably like any other high society woman. Cold. Polite. Angry to find out that she has two illegitimate grandchildren."

"She did send for us," Willow pointed out.

"Duty, not want," Ivy stated. "Mark my words."

The untimely death of their mother six months ago had thrown the girls' lives into chaos. Their mother's small pension from the Paris Opéra Ballet had all but dried up, leaving them bereft of funds while they attempted to finish their dance schooling. Ivy needed just one more year before she was ready to take center stage as a prima ballerina. She had been training all of her life for this moment only to realize her dreams might never come to fruition.

With no skills other than language and dance, the girls were unable to pay rent on their small flat and had been on the brink of eviction. Ivy had stayed up half the night trying to find a way for them to remain in Paris and continue on with their lives, but there was none. They had no immediate family, and no reliable social connections other than a paternal grandmother in England, who quite inconveniently knew nothing of their existence. They were penniless, and Ivy had contacted the Duchess as their last hope. They had almost been thrown out into the streets of Paris to fend for themselves.

The Duchess's response had been swift. She agreed to take the girls in under two conditions: one, they would enter society as ladies and do away with becoming prima ballerinas, and two, they would marry in accordance with her wishes. Were they to accept her offer, the stipulations were non-negotiable.

Ivy had scraped together the last of their funds to book passage on the next ship out of Le Havre bound for Portsmouth, England. The Sinclair sisters packed their meager belongings and set out on a two-day journey toward the port. The trade vessel to England, with very little in the way of comfort, was their home for the next few days. It gave them both more than enough time to ponder how different their lives were about to become.

It was difficult for Ivy to imagine a life without ballet. Ivy and Willow had studied five days a week for five to eight hours a day. Their lives were consumed with dance. As the ship carried them farther from France's shore, Ivy's grasp on her old life slackened. Willow had enjoyed ballet, but did not love it the way Ivy did and was not at all concerned about being thrown into a new world or a new life. Ivy shivered, but not just from the cold.

What would England hold for them? What would it hold for her?

***

Ivy sat demurely and touched a brash red curl of hair as the Duchess's shrewd brown eyes coldly raked over her. Ivy's camel-colored gown was at least three years old, but it was clean if not a tad shabby. Though this was their first meeting, the formidable woman was standoffish and every inch an aristocrat.

"Would you two care for a cup of tea?" The Duchess asked with the barest hint of civility.

"That would be lovely, *merci*," Willow responded nervously. Ivy's sister, two years younger and amiable, had no trouble being agreeable. Ivy, however, was bold and spirited, and intended to show no fear or weakness, sensing the Duchess was a noble adversary.

The tension in the room was as thick as a looming fog.

Once the tea was poured, Ivy and the Duchess looked at each other cautiously. Ivy knew there would be no other course except the Duchess's. She might as well fling herself into the treacherous river and let the current carry her, for swimming upstream would be just as futile as fighting the Duchess.

"How was the journey from Paris?" the Duchess finally asked, slicing into the awkward silence.

"Pleasant, thank you," Willow answered, looking pointedly at her sister to say something.

"Cold," Ivy blurted out.

The Duchess raised her eyebrows and then said briskly, "England is colder than France as a general rule."

Ivy wanted to make a snide remark that the temperature in the drawing room was cooler than outside, but she wisely kept quiet, not believing the Duchess would appreciate her humor.

"Enough about the weather. How old are you?"

"I am nineteen, and Willow is seventeen," Ivy answered.

"Have either you mastered any feminine accomplishments?"

"What do you mean, Your Grace?" Willow asked.

The Duchess did little to hide her exasperation. "Do either of you paint? Play the pianoforte? Sing? Sketch, or press flowers into a book?"

"Pressing flowers into a book is an accomplishment?" Ivy's lips twitched in amusement at the absurdity of the Duchess's comment.

The Duchess's eyes flashed in annoyance, and Willow interjected hastily, "No, Your Grace. We do none of those things. We had tutors growing up, and we are learned in language and history. And of course, we took ballet dance instruction."

I should tell her about my love of fishing and riding horses astride. It might send her into a fit! Ivy thought better of it and wisely kept quiet.

Puckering her lips in clear disapproval, the Duchess stated, "You both are years behind, and lessons in ballroom dancing, polite conversation and etiquette will begin at once. Curtsying and walking in stiff dresses will occur after Madame LaRue, my personal modiste, outfits you for the Season, and because both of you have no feminine skills to your name, I will have painting, singing, and pianoforte instructors come and gauge your potential talent. You will then spend at least four afternoons a week cultivating a basis of civility so that you will at least *appear* to be ladies of the *ton.* Your appearance and background will no doubt shock the members of my circle."

Willow blinked owlishly, and sent Ivy a panic stricken look. Ivy's hand had involuntarily curled into a small fist in her lap, a sign of true distress. The Duchess's words were assaults, beating down all of Ivy's reserves, but apparently there was one more devastating blow to deliver.

"Ballet," the Duchess barked, "will cease."

Rage boiled in Ivy's veins, though she managed to hold her tongue at the Duchess's scornful tone. People of quality had endless amounts of time to groom their daughters into witless mannequins, and it angered Ivy, for she was to become one of them. She had accomplishments more worthwhile, but she was being lectured and ridiculed because she was not able to paint a bowl of fruit. And then to be told that she could no longer continue with her passion was simply too much to bear.

Clamping her jaw shut, Ivy's green eyes narrowed in resentment. She would not give the woman the satisfaction of an outburst, which would only prove Ivy's hoyden tendencies.

"Perhaps you will not be hopeless in society after all," the Duchess intoned loftily, her gaze resting on Ivy. "Dinner will be at eight. Benson will show you to your rooms."

With no choice but to take their leave, the girls rose and moved slowly to the door. Willow stopped abruptly and turned. "Thank you for taking us into your home."

"I am glad at least one of you is diplomatic and pragmatic." The Duchess glanced at Ivy. "It is best not to be ruled by emotions." She looked out the window in resolute dismissal.

"Thank you for my first lesson," Ivy echoed tonelessly. She did not want to be penniless, but being a lady of society did not appeal to her either. She was trapped in the middle of two very different lives. She knew when she booked passage to England that she and her sister would be thrust into a foreign world, a world of guidelines and restrictions, but she had no idea what to expect until now. Her head was a jumbled mess as she left the drawing room and made her way upstairs.

When the Duchess was finally alone, she sighed deeply. She had not expected this at all; a feeling of reluctant admiration and hope was spreading through her. Willow could be molded, but Ivy was already formed. She was forceful and steadfast in her anger. She was magnificent.

She reminded the Duchess so much of herself.

Chapter II

Hampshire, England

A winsome blonde pushed a bottle of fifty-year-old brandy in front of her family's middle-aged butler as he reclined in a scarred wooden chair in the kitchen.

The man had been employed as Lord and Lady Fitzgerald's butler for more than twenty years. He managed to give everyone who came to call the impression that he was upright, good at his job and even happy to do it. Little did they know that Cartwright was easily bribed for sensitive information, and it only took a bottle of good liquor. He seemed to know something about everyone, and footmen and maids rarely spoke in jest around him, afraid he would report everything to the master and mistress of the house.

He was loyal to no one but himself.

"Now, what could this be for?" Cartwright drawled, touching the bottle of brandy.

The young woman's hazel eyes narrowed and she crossed her arms. "You know *what*, Cartwright. Father had a meeting with the Earl of Stanton, and I want to know what happened!" she demanded. She pursed her lips in obvious irritation.

The butler smiled. "Seems to me they were discussing betrothals."

Hazel eyes shifted from sparks of ire to warmth and delight. "Really? Anything else, Cartwright?" she asked hopefully.

He raised an eyebrow. *This woman will make her future husband miserable*, he thought derisively. Though she was beautiful and well bred, she was incredibly spiteful, and when riled she had a temper that rivaled an asp's. She would not make for a welcome bed partner.

"If all goes well, you might find yourself engaged in a few weeks."

Tossing an errant blonde curl over her left shoulder, she haughtily inclined her head and left the kitchen without saying another word. She went to the salon, thinking of her pending engagement. Though it would not do well to get ahead of herself, she did not believe for an instant that it would not come to pass.

Emily sat on a couch with her skirts fetchingly spread around her and opened a book. She hoped to lose herself in it while she waited for her friends to arrive for tea.

She thought of the girls she would ask to be her bridesmaids. Not her cousin, Lucy. She was awkwardly rotund and would throw off the entire bridal party vision. Maybe her cousin Victoria…she was tall and graceful, but not very attractive. She would not steal focus away from Emily during the procession. And then there were the two girls coming for tea, Mathilda and Alyssa. *They would love to be bridesmaids*, Emily thought. *Both would look just a* trifle *washed out in yellow*. She smiled cruelly.

"Miss Mason and Miss Alexander are here, Miss Emily," Cartwright articulated in a perfectly docile tone from the entrance of the salon.

"Send them in, Cartwright."

A moment later, two young ladies entered. After they all exchanged pleasantries and Emily had tea served for them, Mathilda, a petite brunette said, "I understand you are going to Paris for a few weeks?"

Emily nodded. "I am. I will be staying with my favorite aunt for a spell. My parents are allowing me a full French wardrobe for the Season this year."

Alyssa's blue eyes twinkled inquisitively. "Are you leaving soon?"

Emily smiled and shrugged. "Soon enough."

Mathilda and Alyssa exchanged looks. "What does that mean?" Alyssa asked.

Emily took a deep breath and then decided she had to confide in someone, and it might as well be her two closest friends.

"I believe I will leave after my betrothal to the Earl of Stanton is arranged," Emily said simply. She tried not to smile, but an errant grin crossed her face. She was like a cat that had just eaten an entire bowl of cream and had gone back for seconds.

"The Earl of Stanton? *Truly*?" Mathilda cried out, knowing Emily had her heart set on becoming titled.

Emily nodded. "He was here visiting my father this morning."

"He must be on the verge of offering for you," Alyssa agreed.

"Can you imagine? Emily, you are going to be the next Countess of Stanton!" Mathilda said, trying in vain to hide her jealously and obviously doing a poor job of it.

Emily could no longer keep from boasting. Her hazel eyes danced merrily as she blurted, "He has been here to see Father numerous times in the past month!"

Mathilda reached over and grabbed Emily's hand. "Have you thought about your wedding?"

Emily attempted to rein in her satisfaction, but it was difficult. The Earl of Stanton was one of the most eligible bachelors of the year. He had eluded the clutches of numerous young women and their matchmaking mothers, and now Emily was on the verge of becoming his fiancée. *I will have everything I have ever desired,* she thought gleefully.

She would become the Countess of Stanton.

It was all but settled.

***

Cyrus Corbin Archibald, the fifth Earl of Stanton, waited for his solicitor to take a seat across the massive oak desk. Nathan Crosby was barely over five feet tall, yet he managed to convey a formidable presence when he wished. He maintained that rare ability when imparting bad news. Usually admiring of Nathan's talent, at the moment Cy abhorred it, since he was about to be subjected to it directly.

"You cannot continue paying the debt this way, My Lord. If you go on much longer, you will have to sell everything you own. The interest alone is a small fortune," Nathan said, shuffling papers and laying a few on the desk in front of the Earl.

Cy did not even glance at them; he already knew what they said. Looking at them would just annoy him further. "I am aware," Cy voiced blandly, adjusting his long legs in the plush leather chair. He sighed resolutely. "I have no choice but to marry for wealth." The idea made his throat tighten, and his stomach burn.

Nathan Crosby had been the Earl's solicitor since Cy had come of age. Though the title was hundreds of years old and full of prestige, Stanton heirs never seemed to possess any sort of business acumen, including Cy's father. After inheriting the family title, Cy quickly realized that he had the elusive talent for business, and more importantly, he actually enjoyed it.

Unfortunately, Cy did not have the chance to double a stout inheritance. He barely had two pence to scratch together, not to mention the matter of repaying the debt his father had left him, along with hefty interest for such a lengthy delay in remittance.

Only a select few knew of the debt or how it had been incurred, and Nathan Crosby was one of them. The late Earl had borrowed money from the late Duke of Cavehill. The man had a weakness for gambling and cards, but no good fortune. Mortgaged and indebted up to his ears, and with the family estate nearly on the auction block, Cy's father borrowed money to save the family estate for his only son. The Duke of Cavehill died only four years later, and the Earl of Stanton died two years following.

At the age of six and twenty, Cy inherited his title, along with an enormous debt between two men who were no longer living.

Cy vowed to repay the debt, restore the family fortune and marry a woman of quality. These things alone would restore the family title to respect and honor and enable him to finally live the life of a true gentleman.

Possessing a strong desire to right his situation, Cy believed himself completely capable of doing so. Thinking that if he had inherited wealth instead of debt, he would have already tripled his family fortune, but because he was financially crippled by such a colossal debt, Cy could only invest small amounts at certain times, and the returns never came close to matching the interest that was owed. His existing land, estate and investments made him appear to be a wealthy man, but in actuality, he was barely solvent.

It angered him to no end. He pledged that no future generation of his family would suffer from his father's reckless choices. The debt would end with him, even if that meant selling his title on the marriage mart to snag himself a wealthy wife.

Cy's morning had been rotten. First, his favorite stallion slipped a shoe. Then, his perfectly fitted brown jacket sleeve ripped. And now he was forced to discuss marriage plans to prevent imminent financial ruin, almost as if he were discussing the weather with a passerby.

"You could mortgage some of your smaller properties," Nathan suggested. "Or sell your investments in the shipping companies."

Cy shook his head. "Both options are out of the question. I will not do as my father and mortgage my lands, leaving me penniless. If I marry a woman who has a large enough dowry, I can wipe the debt clean, start turning a profit from my existing investments, and build back my rightful wealth. I want this debt cleared without leaving me destitute, landless and with no hope for the future. Besides, it is past time I marry and produce an heir," he stated sardonically.

"Is it to be Miss Emily Fitzgerald then?" Nathan asked, knowing his employer had been spending a great deal of time with the young woman's father.

Cy thought of the attractive blonde. Though she was beautiful and the daughter of a baron, she inspired no deep emotion in him. She would be perfect, but more specifically her dowry would cover his inherited debt in full, including interest. They both would lead separate lives; he had no qualms about shackling himself to a well-bred woman who would act as his hostess and provide him with an heir.

Sitting back in his chair, Cy pressed his fingertips together in thought. "I will send correspondence to Miss Fitzgerald's father. Have the marriage contract drawn up."

"As you wish." Nathan took off his glasses and polished them for a moment in silence. After he put them back on, he looked at Cy and with complete sincerity said, "Congratulations."

Cy smiled ironically. "Thank you, Nathan. You always know just what to say."

***

London, England

Lord Brandon Caldwell stepped off the cobblestone street, adjusted his cravat and straightened his brown overcoat. Walking down Bond Street for a few minutes, he then turned down a narrow alleyway littered with scattered garbage and other refuse. A dirty orphan boy, who was inadequately clad for the English winter, darted out in front of Caldwell. His big, brown eyes pleaded for a handout. Lord Caldwell sniffed in disdain and peered down at the child as if he were vermin. The boy recognized the look and scampered off through soiled snow, glad he had not received the back of the gentleman's hand.

When Caldwell reached the end of the alley, he knocked on a chipped red door, and a moment later a middle-aged woman with a heaving chest and wearing far too much rouge answered. She smiled in greeting and quickly ushered him inside. A dark hallway opened into a large, dimly lit room decorated in red silks and plush brocade.

"Good afternoon, *Monsieur* Caldwell," the woman purred with an engaging smile. "It is such a pleasure to see you. What can I do for you today?"

"Is Angeline available?" Caldwell asked.

Madame Rousard did not care for the pompous gentleman, but he came to her brothel on a regular basis nonetheless. Caldwell paid well in return for clean girls and the utmost discretion. Angeline was available, but it would cost him, and Madame Rousard had no doubt he would pay.

"*Mais oui*, anything for you," she cooed flirtatiously.

Caldwell inclined his head and followed Madame Rousard down the squeaky wooden hallway. Sounds of ecstasy and the scent of heavy perfume filtered through thick doors on either side of the hall. When they came to a dead end, Madame Rousard knocked on a door to the right and opened it.

The room was decorated in pastel lavender and white, and a young woman lay on the bed wearing a white, silk robe. Her long, brown hair was straight and covered one eye. She kept her gaze lowered, her youthful cheeks stained with a woman's first blush.

"Angeline," Madame Rousard announced, glancing at the girl. She knew Lord Caldwell preferred his women on the brink of womanhood. He liked them nubile and young, receiving his cruel pleasure with a feigned cry of desire. The Madame closed the door, a warning knell of what was to come.

He slowly took off his coat and walked towards Angeline. He grabbed her right arm, pulled her towards him forcefully, and then parted her robe and slipped his hands inside. She looked up and watched him with calm eyes, but her heart raced, and he smiled maliciously when he gripped her delicate wrist in a painful grasp.

"Will you beat me again tonight?" Angeline ventured, her voice trembling in a faint Irish lilt.

Madame Rousard had given all her girls French names, claiming that the French were better lovers, hoping men would pay more for their services. Angeline tried not to think of her given name, or her dead parents and brother buried in Ireland, and a life she should have already forgotten. Best to leave it in the past, dead, for there was no hope to ever return to it. She had no one now, except a man whose incredibly handsome face hid his twisted cravings.

He loomed over her, and she knew he anticipated an evening of selfish desire. He was rough and punishing, but Angeline did not have to work for a whole week on what she made in an hour with him. Not that anyone would pay for a battered doxy anyway.

Caldwell did not say a word as he roughly shoved her away from him and began to take off his belt. Angeline tried not to shudder in fear, but she could not help it. The beatings hurt, and she knew he liked it when she cried. She waited expectantly for what was about to happen.

Perhaps Madame Rousard would let her have a new dress, or a box of decadent chocolates if the night went well.

She quaked as he wrapped his belt around his hand and came towards her...

***

Hampshire, England

Ivy could not sleep, tossing and turning like waves in an ocean storm. She was unable to get comfortable in the fluffy feather bed in her elegant bedroom that was the size of their old Paris flat. Though the bed had soft, white satin sheets and was more decadent than anything she had ever slept on, thoughts continued to race through her troubled mind, and the rich food she consumed at dinner settled in her belly like rocks.

Ivy had always been independent and self-reliant, and asking others for aid battered her self-worth. She knew there had been no other option, but the Duchess's steady, unwavering and hostile gaze over dinner left her anxious. Thank God her sister was asleep down the hall. At least the sisters still had each other, for Ivy did not know what she would do if Willow had not been there.

There was a light knock on her door and a moment later Willow popped her head in. "Ivy, are you asleep?"

"Come in, Willow," Ivy answered as she pulled back the covers on her bed and moved to light the candle on the bedside table.

Willow entered the bedroom and closed the door. She quickly climbed into bed next to Ivy. "I have the softest, largest bed in the world, and yet I miss sharing our tiny bed."

Ivy sighed. "I think it will take some time to adjust to our new life." She wondered if she would ever be comfortable in this cold, sheltered world. She felt like a caterpillar, waiting and hoping desperately to become a butterfly, and dreaming of flying away.

"Get up," Ivy said suddenly, throwing off the covers. She drew back the curtain to reveal a full moon. Reaching for her sash, she tied up her nightdress.

"Please do not make me," Willow pleaded.

Ivy chuckled, but pulled Willow off the bed. "How is it you were ever going to be a ballerina? You hate to practice."

Willow shrugged and then tied up her own nightdress. "Perhaps I have more interests than just ballet?"

Ivy looked at her and teased, "You had better not be speaking about pressing flowers into books. Come, let us begin." The sisters began moving through dance positions almost without thought; it was so natural to them. When they finished, they clambered into Ivy's huge upholstered bed. Ivy blew out the candle, and the girls fell asleep.

***

"How did you sleep, Ivy?" Willow asked, her blue eyes wide with sham innocence.

Ivy threw her younger sister a genuine smile and said, "Not as well as you, Willow. You can sleep anywhere."

Willow chuckled. Even after the dance positions, Ivy had a restless night. This morning, she was tired and listless. Willow, on the other hand, seemed to have a never-ending supply of energy, no matter how little sleep she received.

They were as different in dispositions as they were in appearance. Willow looked like their mother. Tall, lithe, blonde and blue-eyed, she was incredibly sweet and feminine. Though she was talented at ballet, she had never been as committed as Ivy.

Ivy had a sharp mind, a clear intellect and incredible spirit. Her small chin jutted out just enough to show a sense of dignity. Her eyes were emerald green and her cheekbones were flawlessly high. She was small in stature and could be mistaken for fragile, but there was a core of strength about her. How else had she managed after their mother died? When she took center stage, all eyes were on her, and it was though she grew three feet in height. She commanded attention.

After breakfast, they walked down the hallway to the drawing room, Willow chattering on like a cheerful little songbird. Ivy listened with one ear as she took in her surroundings, likening the manor to a museum. It was prestigious and large and objects were to be looked at, but not touched. When they arrived at their destination, she smoothed her old blue gown to make sure she was as presentable as possible, not wishing to give the Duchess a reason to snipe at her.

"How are you finding your rooms?" the Duchess asked when the girls were seated. Her tone was full of standard civility, but her face was blank, betraying no lingering emotion.

"Beautiful and capacious. I have never had so much space to myself," Willow replied earnestly. "Thank you so much."

Willow's pleasure did nothing to melt the Duchess's frosty demeanor. "You are welcome." She looked at Ivy. "And you?"

"I am settled," Ivy clipped noncommittally.

The Duchess compressed her lips, no doubt in disapproval of Ivy's intractable iron will. "I am having an informal ball in May to introduce you both to our neighbors. It only gives us two months to make sure you are both presentable. Come June, your official debut will commence in the splendor of London. Balls, theatre, opera…"

The Duchess rang a small brass bell to ring for tea, which was a taciturn affair much like their dinner the previous evening. Willow attempted to break the unrelenting silence a few times, but it was met with vague replies from Ivy and resentful looks from the Duchess. Willow quickly gave up and drank her tea in silence.

***

The next morning after breakfast, Madame LaRue, the Duchess's personal modiste, arrived with two assistants, plenty of measuring tape and a sketchbook. Madame LaRue was less than five feet tall and traveled with a small platform so she could measure all her customers herself. She was of an indiscriminate age, and it was unclear whether she was thirty or fifty. Her face was unlined, except for when she smiled, and then it was as if tiny spider webs had formed at the corners of her eyes. A flurry of energy, she constantly seemed to be in two places at once.

The woman positively radiated excitement at seeing Ivy and Willow; she was overjoyed with Ivy's coloring and Willow's tall frame. "Two lovely sisters. You will both take London by storm!" the woman predicted.

"I am so excited!" Willow twirled in place. "I cannot wait for our new wardrobes. I feel positively shabby!"

It was hard for Ivy to maintain her stoicism when she saw her sister so happy. Though it would take weeks for their clothes to be completed, Willow's pleasure was unrivaled.

After hours of measuring, questioning and incessant chatter from Madam LaRue, Ivy fell exhaustedly into a chair. She did not think she had the stamina, or the desire to be a lady. She looked at the Duchess and said, "Please tell me I do not have to do this again for a very, very long time."

The Duchess's resolute face did not change when she replied, "Not until next season."

Ivy was unable to stifle a groan.

Willow grinned, despite the Duchess's reserved manner, and said, "I have never had so many beautiful things all at once."

"I do believe you will enjoy London," the Duchess remarked.

"It sounds wonderful," Willow admitted. "Though I doubt Ivy shares my sentiments."

"Though Ivy is stunning, she reminds me of a newborn colt. It will be interesting to see if she will find her way, or fall at the first sign of difficulty." The Duchess spoke of Ivy like she had already vacated the room.

Willow looked at the Duchess in surprise. "You think Ivy is stunning?

"She also compared me to a horse," Ivy said dryly.

Stifling a gurgle of laughter, Willow said, "Ivy would prefer the country to the city. She has more use for a well-crafted fishing rod than ball gowns," Willow teased. The moment she realized what she said, she closed her mouth and sent an apologetic look to her sister.

The Duchess's mouth formed into a tight line of disdain. "You *fish*?"

Ivy was used to scrutiny. In ballet lessons, eyes were always on her. Every step she took had to be precise, her body in perfect form. Any mistake would be pointed out immediately and without hesitation. After Ivy became used to that type of close examination, she knew how to perform under pressure. She employed that skill now, glad that some part of her past could be of use in this new, strange life.

"I *used* to fish, Your Grace," Ivy lied. "When I was younger. I do not anymore."

The Duchess's eyes raked over Ivy, searching for the truth. "Fishing is not ladylike. You will put your mind to learning other more useful skills now, and eventually you will have something to offer a husband."

"Fan waving and polite conversation? Will that prove my value?" Ivy shot out sarcastically, unable to keep silent. In France, men loved women of witty intelligence, but it seemed in England that any stamp of originality was rubbed out at birth.

The Duchess lashed out in contempt, "Right now, young lady, you do not have anything to offer as a high society wife. You have no wealth, no breeding and no feminine accomplishments to your name. What man of quality would ever think to offer for you?"

Ivy's eyes flashed dark green in anger as she rose. "I cannot change my breeding or my wealth. My mother thought it was more important to cultivate a strong mind and character than learn how to paint. One thing I do have is pride. I would not care even if you were Queen of England, I will not sit here and allow you to lecture me on circumstance." Ivy stormed out, leaving Willow alone with the Duchess.

"Your sister has quite the temper," the Duchess said finally.

"Yes, she does." Willow looked at the Duchess with uncertainty.

The Duchess arched a brow. "I think she may survive London after all."

Chapter III

Paris, France, March of 1815

"Would you like another cup of tea, dear?"

Emily smiled at her aunt and replied, "Thank you, Aunt Mildred. Another cup would be lovely."

Even though Mildred made her home in Paris, she was still quite English at heart, and Emily loved staying with her when she visited. After all, Mildred lived in a fashionable district and in a luxurious townhouse that was decorated in vibrant colors.

"I am so glad you are here, Emily."

"You are my favorite aunt, and I am glad I came to visit."

Mildred patted her silver hair and said with a wink, "Especially since you are going to be a married woman soon. I will, of course, travel to England to see you wed. I cannot wait to see you married in all of London's splendor."

"I am excited to begin the wedding preparations."

She did not mention to her aunt that the engagement had yet to run in *The Times*, high society's way of announcing betrothals, but she was confident that it would all go off without a hitch.

"You *must* speak to my modiste. She has the ability to design you the most splendid wedding gown. Every girl who sees you will want one just like it. You will be a sensation!"

Emily smiled to herself, and her mind began to wander. She would become a countess. She tried to remain humble, but it was difficult, especially when she thought of her friends back in England. Neither Mathilda nor Alyssa were engaged yet and the letters she received from them were bland, with no interesting information whatsoever. She pitied them. After all, they were not nearly as beautiful as she was, nor were their fathers as wealthy as hers. He was only a baron, but Emily had class and wealth enough to attract the Earl of Stanton. No doubt her friends would marry men of lesser titles with modest wealth.

The thought of her new dress brought her back to conversation. "I would *love* to meet your modiste, Aunt Mildred."

***

Hampshire, England

Cy read the note from the Dowager Duchess of Cavehill, requesting a meeting immediately. Though it was vague, Cy knew the letter concerned the unresolved debt between their families. He penned a quick reply and gave it to his waiting footman.

He called at two in the afternoon, ready to inform the Duchess of his impending marriage, and to assure her that the money owed would be in her hands in less than a fortnight.

Benson, the Duchess's butler, led Cy to an intimate salon where he admired the rich elegance of the room. When the Duchess entertained, though she had not done so in a few years, no expense was spared; the woman had immaculate taste.

The Duchess rose from her seat when Cy entered, her bearing straight and her mostly silver hair arranged into a neat bun. She was still quite young, he realized.

"Thank you for coming on such short notice, Stanton," the Duchess greeted, her intelligent gaze sliding over his muscled form and height.

"It is my pleasure, Your Grace." He sat and crossed his long legs, waiting for the Duchess to explain why she wanted him to call on her.

"I would like to speak plainly, if I may." Cy nodded in agreement and she went on, "There is an outstanding debt incurred by your father that now rests on your shoulders. I am willing to forgo repayment in full on one condition: you marry my granddaughter."

Cy schooled his face into a blank slate, even though his heart skipped a beat and then resumed a steady rhythm. "I did not know you had a granddaughter."

The Duchess sighed. "I have two. My son had a Parisian mistress that he kept hidden and fathered two children with her."

Cy's mind reeled. It was unusual for anyone in their class to admit to skeletons in the family closet, especially to someone not considered friend or confidant.

"My eldest granddaughter, Ivy Sinclair, wrote me weeks ago asking for my assistance. She and her sister were living in Paris, training to become prima ballerinas. Not long ago, their mother died unexpectedly, and because they have no other living relatives, I sent for them."

"How generous of you. Why are you taking me into your confidence? This is a private family matter."

She folded her hands in her lap. "As you well know, I have not pressed you for full repayment. I simply do not need the money. Marry Ivy and I will relinquish the debt *and* provide her with a dowry."

His eyes narrowed. *Her granddaughter must be a spiteful shrew*, he thought unkindly. Why else would the Duchess offer her granddaughter to him, willingly volunteer to clear the debt *and* bestow a dowry?

"I am engaged to Miss Emily Fitzgerald," Cy stated. The ink was barely dry on the contract, but it was an engagement nonetheless. He would not rescind; he was no scoundrel.

The Duchess stared at him in disbelief. "Then why have I not seen an announcement?"

Touché, he thought. "It has only just been settled," he averred.

"Do you care for Miss Fitzgerald?" the Duchess asked pointedly.

Cy's face remained impassive. "I fail to see how that is any of your concern, nor does it matter."

Surprisingly, the Duchess cackled and responded, "Your deflection answered my question. I loved my husband. We were the darling set of society. Our relationship, though unusual, was envied by all."

"What makes you think I would marry a woman I have not even met?" Cy inquired, skipping over the topic of love. Love was not a necessity, not for his marriage. More so, in his circle, love was mentioned in the same breath as the lost city of Atlantis.

The Duchess inclined her head. "Miss Fitzgerald may be lovely, but she will bore you. Are you marrying her for her dowry?"

"My reasons for marriage do not concern you, Your Grace," he answered in a clipped tone. "Did your husband ever tell you why he lent my father money?"

She shrugged elegantly. "I did not ask William about his affairs. All I knew was that a large sum exchanged hands. After William died, I discovered from the family solicitor how large the debt had grown from lack of payments on interest."

Cy smiled without humor. "Ah, of course. You can thank my father for that."

"This is a reasonable solution. It is rumored by well-respected men that you have a talent for business, but you cannot forge ahead saddled with this debt. Do you not wish to see your wealth restored?"

"At what cost?" Cy brooded. "You are trying to seek a title for your illegitimate granddaughter. Are you trying to buy her way into society? Is she not pleasing to look upon, or perhaps she is a harpy with a vicious streak? Surely there must be someone else who is indebted to you so that you can shackle one of your granddaughters to another titled man, or am I so far in debt that you think I have no other choice?"

The Duchess's face darkened in anger. "Are you so *exceedingly* cold and cynical that you would marry a woman merely for her dowry? If that is all you desire, then why not marry Ivy, or do you also wish for your wife to have noble blood? Miss Fitzgerald is the daughter of a lowly baron. Ivy is the granddaughter of a *duke*, Stanton! The Cavehill line is old and prestigious. Your children can have everything that was meant for them. Your future will be secure. The debt will be cleared, and two powerful families will finally have an alliance."

"You cannot simply buy me, Your Grace. I still have a sense of pride," Cy stated very quietly, his gaze level. "And I highly doubt you are overjoyed to have two reminders of your son's indiscretions living under your roof."

The Duchess flinched as though Cy had reached out and slapped her. "What I feel for my granddaughters is none of your concern. I, too, have pride. You are entitled to yours. I am giving you an out, Stanton. Why not take it? I am not unfeeling towards your plight.

"Your father was not shrewd with financial matters, but pride never entered his mind when he thought of asking my husband for money to save the land and estate that has become *your* inheritance."

She was presumptuous and self-righteous, but she was correct. *Damn the woman!* Cy thought irritably.

"At least meet Ivy before you dismiss the idea of marrying her. You will see she is neither homely, nor mean spirited."

Cy sighed and finally relented to the battle of wills. "As you wish, Your Grace. I will meet your granddaughter." It would do no harm, though he doubted he would be swayed from his course of marrying Miss Fitzgerald.

The Duchess rang her brass bell, and a moment later a maid entered. "Please bring Miss Ivy to the salon." The maid curtsied and left. "Miss Fitzgerald does not have the fire you need, Stanton. Your life will be dull and empty with her as your wife."

Cy's mouth quirked in amusement. "And your granddaughter is…?"

Before the Duchess could reply, a musical voice asked from the doorway, "You requested my presence, Your Grace?"

Turning slowly, the breath left Cy's lungs. The woman who stood at the entrance to the salon was simply stunning. She was petite with flawless, porcelain skin, high cheekbones and emerald green eyes that gazed at him speculatively. Her hair was a mass of molten, titian waves that fell all the way to the middle of her back. Cy's gray eyes roved appreciatively over her, settled for a moment on her plush, pink lips and then drifted back to her face. He rose immediately, unfolding his long frame from his seat.

She was staring at him with nothing more than courteous interest, and suddenly he wished to see her eyes darken with passion. He was completely caught off guard by his own desire.

"Ivy, this is our neighbor, the Earl of Stanton," the Duchess introduced plainly.

Ivy turned to him and fell into a graceful curtsy. He crossed to her, took her hand in his and kissed it. She rose, and craned her neck to look at him. She was so delicate, and he was well over six feet. He towered over her, enjoying the hesitancy in her eyes, as if she did not know what to make of him.

Though she obviously attempted to conceal her emotions, she did not win the conflict. She was so expressive, and he enjoyed the fact that she did not appear aloof. Instantly, he knew she was not like other young ladies her age that simpered and acted coy.

"It is a pleasure to meet you, My Lord," she murmured.

"Miss Sinclair, your grandmother has told me such wonderful things about you." He noticed her disbelieving glance in the Duchess's direction, and raised a mocking eyebrow.

Ivy responded glibly, "Her Grace is the epitome of hospitality and generosity."

"How is your dance lesson coming along?" the Duchess interjected quickly.

"Well. It is one area where I excel. If you will excuse me, I would like to get back to it." Ivy curtsied again and then left in a swish of blue muslin.

Cy leisurely turned back to the Duchess and began to smile slowly. "I should have given you more credit, Your Grace. You missed your calling. You could have been an agent against Napoleon for all *your* skill in battle."

The Duchess raised her eyebrows and inclined her head in salute. "She is spirited, Stanton. It must be a quality of their mother. Her sister, though different in appearance, shares some of the same characteristics."

"*Dear God*," Cy breathed. "I forgot there was another one. Why did you insist that I meet Ivy and not her sister?"

The Duchess spoke candidly, "Willow will no doubt enjoy the excitement of courting in London, and as beautiful and charming as she is, she will have no lack of suitors, but Willow accidently divulged that Ivy would much prefer to fish than wave a fan. She needs to be with a man that appreciates pluck, Stanton. Ivy is headstrong and willful, but she listens to reason. Do not let the circumstances of her birth sway your decision. I saw the way you reacted to her. Given some time, I believe you will both come to an agreement that suits us all."

Cy looked at the Duchess with skepticism. "Will your granddaughter agree to my suit?"

The Duchess set her cup of tea down and said, "I have made it quite clear that the girls will marry in accordance with my wishes, but I have not informed Ivy of my decision to make a match between the two of you."

They stared at each other for a long moment. Finally Cy nodded and said, "I will extract myself from Miss Fitzgerald post haste. However, I want a few weeks, perhaps even a month with Miss Sinclair so that we might get to know each other."

"As you wish. I am throwing a ball for the girls in May to introduce them to the rest of our neighbors. You will of course be in attendance."

"I would not miss it. I am sure it will be a most diverting evening," he replied politely.

***

Paris, France

Emily gripped her hands tightly to keep from reaching for one of Aunt Mildred's small glass figurines on the fireplace mantle. She wanted nothing more than to pick one up and throw it against the wall and hear its fragile body shatter.

The Earl of Stanton had broken their engagement, and she did not have the faintest idea why. *I am beautiful, well-bred and would make any man a perfect wife*, she thought loftily. Yet here she was, sitting in Aunt Mildred's drawing room hearing from her father that her betrothed had cried off, tossing her aside like rotting vegetable one throws out with the refuse.

There had been no repercussions.

"Em, kitten, you must look at the bright side," her father soothed, ignoring her glare. "At least he broke the engagement off *before* it was announced. No one has to know."

"Why did you come here?" she demanded angrily. "I could just as easily have read about it in one of your letters."

He sighed. "I had business to attend to, and I thought it only fitting to be the bearer of bad news in person."

"Perhaps if we had immediately sent the announcement to *The Times* none of this would have happened! You claim he is a gentleman, but no gentleman would do this! He is a lying, deceitful coward! This is *your* fault!"

Fitzgerald shook his head regretfully. "Now Emily, you do not know all the reasons behind his decision. Marriage is a business, my dear. You will see, when you are engaged to someone with an even greater title. Trust me. I will find you someone else. Would you like that?"

She crossed her arms and seethed as her father rose and swiftly retreated. Finally succumbing to her rage, she picked up one of her aunt's delicate glass swan collectibles and threw it against the wall as hard as she could. It gave a resounding crash, but did nothing to appease her anger.

Chapter IV

Hampshire, England

A few ready-made outfits, including riding habits for Willow and Ivy were delivered the day before to the Duchess's home. Willow had jabbered excitedly while holding up different gowns, marveling at the expense and construct. Ivy was glad to have a riding habit. Ever since she stepped foot in England, she had been relegated to the confines of the manor. She yearned for the freedom of galloping across the countryside on the back of a mount. She had chances to ride outside Paris in her very limited spare time, and she had loved every minute of it. The feeling of air being forced into her lungs and the wind whipping through her hair while galloping on a fast mare made her feel alive and carefree.

The late winter morning was unusually sunny as Ivy made her way to the stables. She was impressed by the choices of mounts and horses, and chose a spirited gray mare with snowy white feet named Moonlight.

"I shall saddle her right away for you, Miss Ivy," the groom said.

Ivy shook her head. "That will not be necessary." She took the reins from the groom and quickly mounted the horse despite her cumbersome green skirts.

The groom was scandalized. "You cannot ride without a saddle!"

Ivy grinned at the younger man's wide eyes and astonished face.

"I can and I will," she said confidently. "I have spent many hours cultivating such a skill. I can control a mount perfectly well while riding this way." She would not have *every* freedom renounced. She refused to give up all the things she loved, and would not forget the girl she used to be. She practiced ballet at night in the privacy of her room, but without a real bar and studio, it felt sloppy.

"At least let me escort you," the groom sputtered.

She shook her head, causing the red curls to bounce playfully under her dark green riding hat. "I am staying on Cavehill land. Which way is the little stream I saw on my journey here?"

The groom wanted to protest, but one smile and a shake of Ivy's pretty head threw him into such confusion that he gave in and pointed the way. After receiving directions, she took off across the hill and drew in deep breaths as she rode. The cold breeze whipped through her hair and flushed her cheeks pink. Her spirits soared. Ivy missed having time to herself. She liked not having to worry about judgmental eyes speculating whether or not she was becoming a 'perfect lady.' If anyone saw her now, they would realize it was all a veneer, and she was very much a hoyden.

Half a mile later, she reached the small stream, and the sound of trickling water was soothing to her ears. She had to admit that though she missed Paris, she was beginning to enjoy the acres of space in the English countryside.

She dismounted and tied Moonlight to a nearby tree, and then wished she had thought to bring a blanket so she could sit on the grass without soiling her newly made clothes. She made do with standing along the bank, watching the stream carry dead leaves and twigs along its meandering, dribbling path.

Ivy yearned for spring, and noticed signs all around her that it was on its way. Trees were showing the barest hints of life and animals were poking their heads out of their burrows. She, too, felt like she was shaking off the sleepy, somber winter, her spirit blooming with the coming spring.

Lost in her own thoughts she did not hear a solitary rider approach. The sound of boots on grass startled her. In annoyance, she turned to see who interrupted her solitude. Her displeasure evaporated and a thrill shot through her when she recognized the handsome face.

It was the Earl of Stanton.

His dark brown hair was perfectly cut, yet mussed from riding, his strong jaw cleanly shaven. Garbed in a crisp, white shirt and tan riding breeches that fit him snuggly, she also could not help but notice his tailored riding coat that spanned the wide breadth of his shoulders. She wondered if she could see her reflection is his polished boots; the Earl looked every bit like the titled gentleman he was.

"Good morning," he greeted, his warm gray eyes perusing her. "I am sorry if I distressed you."

She shook her head, sending her red curls over her shoulder. "I am startled to see anyone else awake this early in the morning."

He smiled. “I like early morning rides, too. May I join you?” When she nodded, he came to stand next to her.

“I thought I was on Cavehill land.”

“You are. The Cavehills are allowed to ride on Stanton land, and the Stantons are allowed on Cavehill land.”

“That is an interesting agreement. How did that occur?” She peered at him from beneath heavily fringed eyelashes.

“Well,” he began, “years and years ago, the Duke of Cavehill and the Earl of Stanton had a land-border dispute. There was a lake that fell in the middle of their properties and neither one of them wanted to give it up to the other.”

“Where is the lake?” Ivy wondered.

The Earl grinned down at her. “For a long time no one knew. It just seemed to have disappeared. Each family blamed the other, and it was a source of mystery for the longest time. After years of discord between their families, the Cavehill heir and the Stanton heir joined forces and had the lake filled. Then, each one helped the other build a lake on each sect of land so future generations would have nothing to quibble about. Peace between families has existed ever sense.”

The Earl picked up a small pebble and threw it in the stream. “I would be glad to show you Stanton Lake one day, if you would like.”

“That would be lovely,” she answered tentatively. “Is the lake habitable for fish?”

“It is.”

“Do you fish?”

He smiled. "I do."

She caught her breath; his smile was doing funny things to her stomach. It was like a swarm of flying insects had taken flight inside of her. She was nervous and desperately wanted to escape his presence for fear of committing a verbal blunder. Ivy turned away from the stream and walked to her tethered horse.

"Excuse me, My Lord, I must be getting back."

He bowed. "A pleasure seeing you again, Miss Sinclair."

As she rode off, Cy took a long moment to watch her on the mare, so light and elegant but commanding. Only after a long moment of appreciation did he realize she was riding astride without a saddle. Intrigued, hc wanted to know where she had acquired such a skill.

***

As Ivy was finishing her breakfast, Simms, the footman, entered the dining room and announced, "You have a visitor, Miss Ivy."

"Who is it?" she asked in confusion.

"The Earl of Stanton. His Lordship is waiting for you in the salon."

Ivy stood up slowly. *What is he doing here?* The handsome man made her nervous, and she was in danger of babbling when in his presence. Hesitantly, she walked towards the salon, paused outside the room and took a deep breath before entering.

The Earl was standing by the window, watching the rain descend in thick sheets. His shoulders were broad and seemed to hinder the small amount of light that had managed to break through the ominous, dark sky.

"Good morning," she greeted softly.

The Earl turned at the sound of her voice and smiled. "You look lovely. That color brings out your eyes."

It was such a simple compliment, and it made Ivy feel like she was wearing the most glamorous ball gown in all of England, instead of a light green day gown. She blushed at the warmth in his voice.

He took a few steps towards her, grasped her hand in his and kissed it. His breath grazed her skin, causing nearly imperceptible shivers to race up and down her spine.

"I am sorry for calling without an appointment," he said in a deep, masculine voice.

"Not a problem at all," she replied, striving for calm.

"I am not bothering you, I take it?"

"Would it matter if you were?" she teased.

He laughed. "Absolutely not."

"The longer you are here, the shorter my pianoforte lesson will be. Feel free to stay all day if you like."

"You really hate the pianoforte?" he asked with a smile.

She had the grace to look embarrassed. "Perhaps if I was naturally adept at playing the pianoforte, I might enjoy it. The Duchess insists on adding a few feminine accomplishments to my name, and so far I have tried my hand at painting, the pianoforte and flower pressing."

"And what is the consensus?"

"I am the best at flower pressing, for it requires not a bit of talent!"

He chuckled. "I enjoy your wit, Miss Sinclair. Her Grace wants to ensure you have all the benefits of a genteel lady."

Ivy shrugged her shoulders. "It would be much easier if she realized I have no desire to cultivate such skills, but alas, we are forced into a battle of wills, one I fear I am losing."

"Do you not think those accomplishments are worthwhile?" he asked.

She looked at him plainly and said, "My mother never wasted time on such trivial things, and my father never seemed to care."

"Your mother was not a lady of the gentry," the Earl remarked baldly.

Her green eyes narrowed. "How do you know about my mother?" Ivy's usually unguarded face formed into a disinterested, closed mask, shutting him out.

"Ah," he admitted sheepishly. "Your grandmother confided in me."

Ivy was quiet for a long moment. "I gather she also told you my mother was my father's mistress?"

He nodded sharply, his jaw clenching.

"If you will excuse me, My Lord, my instructor is waiting for me." She turned to leave.

"Miss Sinclair," he called out. "I apologize for my candidness. It was not my intention to insult you."

She nodded her head in acceptance of apology, but she remained cautious. Ivy would never forget the choices her mother made; it seemed society would not either.

"I suppose I should appreciate your honestly."

"I do not wish to cause you distress, Miss Sinclair, nor would I want you to be surprised if you encounter any censure from any future encounters with men and women of my circle."

She smiled though it held no warmth. "Men will not see me as anything more than the pitiful offspring of a French courtesan. Women will laugh behind my back and call me a gauche pretender. I am not so naïve, My Lord."

"Perhaps some of them will surprise you."

"Like you, sir? *Au revoir.*" She left in a rage.

Insufferable cad! Ivy thought angrily as she stomped to her bedroom. *How dare he make me feel less than what I am? How dare I let him!*

Ivy was angry with herself for falling into the handsome man's trap. She would not be so foolish again. She would keep her distance, remind herself that he was a snooty aristocrat and not entertain any ridiculous ideas that they could be friends. Stanton was a good example of what she would face in London, and she best be prepared for it.

***

"I am engaged," Cy announced without preamble as he swirled his brandy around in a crystal snifter. He was sitting in his best friend's library enjoying the roaring fire and his drink.

"Congratulations, I suppose, although you do know how I feel about Miss Fitzgerald," Marcus Fielding, the Count of Langley replied.

Langley and Cy had been close friends since their school days, and Langley was privy to Cy's need for a wealthy wife to cover the debt left by his father. Like his friend, Langley had been heir to a prominent title. Unlike Cy, however, he never had to worry about a dissolving inheritance. He was wealthy and at one time offered to help Cy out of his predicament. Due to Cy's enormous pride, he rejected his friend's assistance. He would not have been able to look Langley in the eye; this was his wrong to right.

"No, not Miss Fitzgerald."

Langley raised his eyebrows. "I am overjoyed. She is beautiful, but she is incredibly banal. Who is the lucky young lady that will become the next Countess of Stanton?"

"Did you want to get married?" Cy asked, ignoring the question.

"No man wants to get married," Langley deflected.

"Your wife is lovely. A woman of substance, intelligence and humor."

"I did not know you held Elizabeth in such high esteem," Langley joked. "She also has remarkable candor. She is a wonderful wife and an incredible mother." The love he felt for his wife and two-year-old son, Malcolm, was evident in his tone of voice.

Cy threw a look at his friend. "Ivy is the same type of woman as your wife."

"Ivy? Intriguing name. I do not recall a woman named Ivy in society."

"She has not been presented." Cy went on to tell Langley about Ivy's background and the proposition the Duchess of Cavehill had presented to him.

Cy raised his glass for a toast. "To Ivy Sinclair, my future wife, who has no knowledge whatsoever of our coming betrothal."

"This will make for an interesting courtship," Langley remarked as he threw back his entire glass of brandy.

"Indeed. And at the moment I have angered the woman and seek to alter it."

Langley raised his eyebrows. "Why is she angry?"

Cy looked chagrined. "I thoughtlessly insulted her *and* her mother in one fell swoop."

"Might I suggest jewels? They do wonders when my wife is cross with me," Langley said with sardonic amusement.

"I doubt Ivy will ever accept bribes."

"Is she so very different then?"

Cy nodded. "She is. There is something about her, Langley. At first, I only noticed her physical beauty, but she has wit and spirit. She is graceful, in a way that I have never seen before. It is as if she understands her own body's movements."

Langley raised an eyebrow. "Careful, man, you sound like you are about to spout a sonnet."

"Do not be an ass." Cy snorted.

"I cannot wait to meet this woman who has you running towards the altar," Langley quipped.

Chapter V

Hampshire, England

After the painting instructor departed, Ivy was granted a few spare moments of reprieve. She sat in the corner of the library with her legs curled underneath her, a crackling fire keeping her warm. She had just begun reading a compilation of Molière's greatest plays when the door opened. She looked up. The Earl of Stanton materialized in the doorway.

She had to stop her hands from flying to her untamable curls. Her stocking clad feet were devoid of slippers, and she hated that she looked less than perfect. Quickly putting on her slippers, she forced her features to remain impassive. He was a snob and she should not care what he thought of her appearance. Their last encounter had ended in verbal sparring, leaving her angry.

"Good afternoon, Miss Sinclair. I always seem to be interrupting you." His tone was pleasant and his gaze warm.

She shut her book. "Good afternoon," she said, rising.

"What are you reading?"

"Molière," she answered, setting the book aside.

"In *French*?"

She nodded. "Of course. I did grow up in Paris, after all. Besides, in English some of the quips are lost. The translation simply will not do."

The Earl shook his head. "Poor Molière. I wonder if he rolls over in his grave thinking of the English ruining all his plays."

"Undoubtedly."

He chuckled. "I brought you a small present."

"A present for me?" she asked quizzically.

"I wanted to make amends for the other day," he explained as he handed her a small package wrapped in nondescript brown paper. "I am sorry for my behavior."

She reached out to take it, wondering what it would cost her. "I can no more change the color of my hair than I can the circumstances of my birth. I will not apologize for it," she said quietly.

"I appreciate your honesty, Miss Sinclair." His tone was sincere.

She looked into his eyes. "You do?"

"Absolutely. It is refreshing to hear someone speak so candidly."

"I grew up in a world where speaking openly was revered, not reviled, My Lord. I am simply too old to curtail my unusual character."

"How old would that be, Miss Sinclair?" He smiled.

She did not answer his question directly when she said, "I have seen much in my short life. More than most young women my age and certainly more than the other young ladies who will become my acquaintances."

"Acquaintances? Not friends?"

"I will not hold out hope that the ladies I encounter will accept me. They, too, will judge me."

He winced. “Can we be friends? I would like to put everything behind us so that we may start anew.”

Her breath caught as she looked up into his inscrutable gray eyes. After a long moment, she nodded. “It is forgotten,” she said softly, and then turned her attention back to the wrapped package. She ripped it open like an excited child.

“*A Gentleman’s Guide to Fishing*?” she breathed with pleasure. “Wonderful! I have been wanting to read it!”

“I had a feeling you might.”

“How did you know I would enjoy this?” she asked, her face lit with delight as she turned over the book and lovingly examined its cover.

“Your grandmother mentioned your love of fishing briefly in conversation.”

A worried look crossed her face. “You do not find it unfeminine?”

“I find it enthralling that we share the same hobby.”

She looked at him intently. When she detected no fabrication, she allowed a glow of warmth and comfort to spread through her. Did all gentleman of quality pay attention to such details?

“Thank you,” she replied. “I will devour it at my earliest opportunity.”

“May I ask you a question?” he asked.

“Of course.”

“The day by the stream, I noticed you did not ride with a saddle. How did you acquire such a skill?”

Her cheeks flamed. “I learned to ride from the owner of a traveling circus. Years ago, *Maman* took us to see the performances, and I vowed to learn to ride without a saddle like the women in the show. They stood on top of a moving mount, of course, but they also rode astride without a saddle."

"Can you stand on top of a moving mount?" the Earl asked in surprise.

Ivy shook her head. "No. I was training to be a ballerina, you see, and I could not risk injuring myself. I settled for learning how to ride without a saddle."

He opened his mouth to reply but then shut it again.

"You think I am a hoyden without hope of becoming a lady," Ivy accused. "I suppose I can hardly blame you."

"No, you misunderstand my silence, Miss Sinclair. Your incredible spirit delights me. You are an outrageous, irreverent little imp."

It was her turn to be speechless as his gaze turned warm and assessing. Ivy's smile wavered at his boldly intimate look. He took a step closer to her, and Ivy instantly darted around him.

"Thank you for the book!" she squeaked and then scurried out the door wishing to put space between herself and the Earl and the desire she felt for him.

***

Two days later, while the Duchess and her granddaughters were eating breakfast, Simms entered the dining room.

"A package has arrived for Miss Ivy," he announced.

"What can it be? Madame LaRue has sent over the last of our wardrobes already," Ivy murmured even as she rose and excused herself.

The Duchess attempted not to show any curiosity, but Willow could not contain her eagerness to discover what Ivy had received, and more importantly, *who* had sent it to her.

Ivy stared at the long and thin package wrapped in brown paper, resting on the chaise in the drawing room. She plucked the small white note that accompanied the gift and read it.

"Perhaps you would like to practice with this once you have finished *A Gentlemen's Guide to Fishing*. My well-stocked lake is open to you whenever you wish." It was signed simply, 'Cy'.

The informality of his signature did not pass unnoticed. They had barely been introduced, but familiarity was growing between them. Slowly, she unwrapped the gift and stared at the most beautiful fishing rod she had ever seen. It was dark wood, hand crafted and a true work of art. The rods she used growing up were rudimentary, and little more than sticks with a line and handmade hook. She had done moderately well, and the local boys told her she was a natural. Fishing with this rod would be different.

"Ivy," Willow breathed coming into the room. "A fishing rod? My, it is breathtaking, even though I abhor the sport! Who is it from?"

"The Earl of Stanton," Ivy answered through a tight throat. She was in awe, but then it quickly turned to nervousness. Was he pursuing her?

"That was very generous of him," Willow replied. She looked at Ivy, who was lost in thought. "You must send him a note."

"Yes. That would be the appropriate thing to do." Ivy sat down at the Duchess's walnut writing desk and picked up the ink quill and a piece of stationary. She wrote a note, the contents of which she refused to share with Willow, and then sealed it with wax. She rang the bell for Simms, and he entered promptly.

"Please take this to the Earl of Stanton," she commanded.

As soon as the note was on its way, Ivy said to Willow, "If you will excuse me, I think I will go for my morning ride."

Willow watched in amazement as Ivy left the room in a swish of muslin. *Does Ivy not wish to receive gifts from the handsome Earl*? Willow wondered. It could not be because of the Duchess who surely approved of Stanton's pursuit. The Earl was a well-bred, eligible bachelor. It would be the grandest match of the Season if an illegitimate daughter of a duke married an earl.

Unable to contain her inquisitiveness a minute longer, the Duchess entered the drawing room. Immediately she noticed the fishing rod, and pursed her lips in disapproval at the unladylike gift.

"A fishing rod? It seems your sister is extremely well suited to the Earl." Her tone was censorious.

Willow nodded. "So it would seem. Will you excuse me? I have a few things I would like to take care of before my dance lesson."

"Willow," the Duchess called. "Most young women would be happy to catch the Earl of Stanton's attention."

"Ivy is not like most women."

"She will have to marry," the Duchess reminded, her usually stoic face softening. "As will you."

"I know."

"You both will cause quite a stir when you enter society. If Ivy can land Stanton, it will make your debut easier."

Willow looked at the Duchess. "I did not think you cared if we had an easy time of it or not."

"I see your sister's penchant for speaking her mind is catching."

Smiling wryly, Willow replied, "I realize we are both uncomfortable reminders of your son's secret life, and I know we have thrown your world into disarray by being here. I am empathetic to your plight, however, a small measure of warmth from you might help us all."

The Duchess raised her eyebrows. "Is that all it would take for you to explain why Ivy is reluctant to accept gifts from the Earl?"

Willow debated on the matter. Their father had been a member of the aristocracy, seducing their mother with charm and rugged good looks. They had met when the Duke had taken a trip to Paris and attended a ballet. From the first moment their mother danced across the stage, the Duke had been entranced.

He had wooed her with compliments and tokens of affection, but never hid the fact that he was married. Despite her better judgment, their mother fell in love with him. Their times together were always brief; he had a real family, after all, back in England. Ivy vowed never to follow the same painful path.

"Ivy has pride, Your Grace. To her, gifts are a consolation prize for something she can never have."

The Duchess frowned. "I do not understand. Stanton is courting her."

"Perhaps Ivy wonders to what end," Willow stated. "Our mother accepted gifts because that was all our father could ever offer her. He could not give her his name or title."

"Ah," the Duchess remarked in understanding.

"Please do not let Ivy know I shared this confidence with you, Your Grace." Willow looked beseechingly at the older woman.

The Duchess inclined her head regally. "My lips are sealed, Willow. Best let this play out between Stanton and Ivy."

***

The next morning, the ladies dined together in relative quiet, which was not unusual. Tea and meals were tense and uncomfortable. Willow brushed aside the strain, babbling away, pretending that one word answers from Ivy and the Duchess was nothing unusual. She often carried the conversation herself.

Today was no different as they sat at a large wooden table, and a footman stood in the corner, ready to serve them tea from an old, but immaculate silver tea set. The walls were paneled oak, and dark red carpet lined the floorboards of the room. Unlit silver candelabras that would easily dispel the darkness of evening graced the table.

Entering the dining room, Simms announced there was another gift from the Earl of Stanton for Miss Ivy in the drawing rom. Willow and the Duchess followed her, unable to hide their interest.

It was a stack of *all* of Molière's work, first editions. Books were terribly expensive, even for the wealthy, and to have a first edition of even *one* of Molière's works was more than Ivy could imagine.

The Earl's gifts were speaking to her heart. He was not buying her jewels or furs, which would appeal to other women. He was spending time thinking of each gift, finding the perfect fit for Ivy, gifts he knew *she* would enjoy. She felt truly pursued and completely out of her element.

"The man is courting you!" Willow squealed. "Why are you not more excited?"

Ivy looked at Willow, and then at the Duchess for confirmation. "Is this true?"

"It would appear so," the Duchess answered.

"Is this not what you wished for all along? A high-class gentleman courting your illegitimate granddaughter?"

"Must you be so mocking and irreverent?" the Duchess demanded angrily.

"Yes, I must!"

Ivy stormed out of the room, wondering if there was anything she could do to please the stern Duchess. And then Ivy wondered why she cared.

***

"Miss Ivy, you have *another* gift," Simms announced in exasperation a week later.

What could it possibly be now? she wondered. Ivy was curled up on a chaise, *A Gentleman's Guide to Fishing* in her lap, but she was much too distracted to read.

"Where is it?" Ivy asked.

"In the stables."

Moments later they were at the Duchess's stables and a groom held the reins to a beautiful black mare with a snowy white patch on her forehead. Her black mane was long and glossy, and she neighed in greeting upon Ivy's arrival. The horse tossed her head impatiently.

"We seem to be very similar," Ivy murmured to the horse, stroking the animal's nose. When she stopped petting it for only a moment, the mare bumped its head against Ivy's hand. Ivy laughed.

"Shall I fetch you ink and paper for a response?" Simms asked.

"That will not be necessary." She grasped the spirited mare's reins and hauled herself up onto the back of the unsaddled animal, sitting astride.

"Miss Ivy!" Simms gasped. He was blushing at the sight of Ivy's legs. "You cannot ride astride. It is unladylike! Do something!" He looked at the groom for help.

"It is best not to fight, Miss Ivy," the groom said, shaking his head. "You will not win."

Ivy's lips quirked into an amused smile. "I cannot control my horse riding sidesaddle. I tried it the other morning and the experience was thoroughly miserable."

The footman sputtered with indignation. "The Duchess will have my head if she discovers I let you leave the stable without a saddle."

"Then do not tell her," Ivy suggested.

Willow had just made her way to the stables, and when she saw Ivy, she gasped.

Simms sighed in relief. "Excellent. Miss Willow, can you talk some sense into your sister?"

"Absolutely not," Willow remarked with a smile. "I was gasping in awe of the mare. Is *that* your gift?"

Ivy nodded. "This is the most extravagant gift I have ever received. I must thank him in person. Which way is the Earl's home?" Ivy asked Simms, who was still attempting to recover from shock.

Simms looked at the groom, as if seeking safety in numbers and then said forcefully, "Miss Ivy, we cannot let you ride this way. Think of the Earl. What will he say?"

Willow smothered her laughter when Ivy's face flushed in annoyance. "I encountered the Earl the other morning, and he saw me riding astride. He called me spirited and unique!" When no one responded, she went on, "Are you and the rest of the staff not *incredibly* loyal?"

"Of course we are," Simms answered, perplexed.

"Then you will ensure discretion. We can be assured the Earl will do the same."

Simms sighed, and Ivy knew she had won. He apparently already recognized Ivy's stubborn expression because he relented and gave her directions to the Earl of Stanton's estate. Ivy turned her mare, and gently brought her to a canter.

"Say hello to the Earl of Stanton for me!" Willow laughingly called as Ivy raced off into the distance.

Why Ivy arrived at the Earl's estate, she did not know where the stables were, so she tied the mare to an iron post near the front of his impressive manor. She rapped on the front door, and the butler answered.

"I am Miss Sinclair," Ivy announced.

The butler blinked several times and then said, "Welcome, Miss Sinclair. Please come in."

"Thank you." As she entered the Earl's home, she took in her surroundings, which consisted mostly of dark, well-crafted wood and luxurious oil paintings. The butler escorted her down the hall, paused outside a closed door, and then knocked on it twice in rapid succession. He waited for a reply from within before opening the door.

The Earl of Stanton rose from his high-backed leather chair and gazed at Ivy across his massive oak desk. "Miss Sinclair, this is a nice surprise," he said with a smile.

"I am not disturbing you, am I?"

"Not at all." He gestured for her to sit down in the chair across from his desk. The butler retreated and closed the door.

Ivy made herself comfortable and stared at him for a moment in silence. "Thank you for the gift."

The Earl grinned. "Which gift would that be?"

"The mare."

"Ah." He leaned back in his chair. "Do you like her?"

"Very much, but I cannot keep her." Her troubled gaze sought his.

"Of course you can. You kept the other gifts," he pointed out wryly.

Ivy sighed in exasperation. "If that is the logic, then I will be returning the other gifts to you as well."

"You do not return gifts. That is the entire point of a *gift*. You are meant to keep and enjoy them."

"You gave me a *horse*," Ivy said in an accusatory tone.

"So I did," he agreed good-naturedly.

"It is extravagant."

He shook his head. "No, it is not. If I had given you the Crown Jewels, that would have been extravagant."

Her eyes were wary. "You are not planning on giving me jewels...are you?"

The Earl's gray eyes were warm. "Would you like it if I did?"

Ivy was vexed, but only because she desperately wanted to hide her growing weakness for the man's charms. "No! I mean, yes. Of course! What woman would not want jewels from you?" She bit her lip.

"Why are you upset?" he asked quizzically.

She looked at his desk, refusing to meet his gaze. "Men only give women gifts when they are interested in earning their affections. You cannot possibly want mine." When he did not respond she looked up to find him closely examining her.

"Why would I not want your affections?" he asked.

She sighed. "You are an earl and I...I am not from the same social circle as you. I did not have the same upbringing."

"Does your grandmother find me unsuitable?" he asked rhetorically.

"Highly unsuitable," she teased before sobering. "You are popular and eligible. I am not suitable for *you*."

"You are going to have to wed, Ivy," he said with familiarity.

She pulled back her shoulders and prickly said, "You were not given permission to use my given name."

He shrugged. "I gave you permission to use mine, I thought it only justifiable to call you by yours."

She tossed her head haughtily. "Presumptuous."

"Indeed." He peered at her. "Would you consider me an option?"

"Consider you?"

"For marriage," he clarified.

"No!" she said quickly.

"Why not?"

"Because you cannot consider *me*! Perhaps if I found a man with a lower title I would not feel so...If you marry me, you will be marrying far below your station and you know it. You cannot ignore the fact that I am not a lady."

"A lady is not always born a lady, Ivy. You have strength in character, the confidence to speak your mind, and an engaging spirit. You are not like other young ladies who were bred into their positions; you are different. But you are still very much a lady." He smiled. "The Duchess would be quite pleased if we married."

"You seem to be the only one who enjoys my dissimilarities. I am sure the Duchess feels as though I should hold my tongue and keep my temper hidden. She has shown me nothing but disdain."

"Perhaps she is trying to teach you a lesson."

"What do you mean, My Lord?"

"If you do not show how the Duchess's cool reception effects you, I imagine there will be nothing in society that you cannot overcome."

"You make a valid point," she murmured. She had not thought about it that way.

"Do you really have no idea of your own worth? Do not let anyone make you feel inferior, even the Duchess."

She scoffed. "I do not feel inferior, sir."

"Cy," he corrected. "And you do feel inferior, otherwise you would not be spouting this nonsense about not being good enough for me. Women usually see me as nothing more than an uncommonly handsome man with a lofty title—one that could better elevate them closer to the pinnacle of society. For as long as I can remember, a woman has never been concerned about what was best for me. Do you really not care for my title? Could you care for me, as a woman cares for a man?"

She stared at him in dazed amazement. "Your frankness astounds me."

"So we have already established." He gazed at her a moment and then asked, "Do you play cards?"

Momentarily taken aback, she replied, "Yes."

"Good." He opened a desk drawer and withdrew a brand new deck, and peeled off the duty wrapper. "Have you ever heard of wagering?"

Alarm bells sounded in her head. Mutely, she nodded. She had heard stories of gentlemen and their gambling clubs; full of sorry chaps who lost everything in a series of bad wagers. Desperate men were even known to wager their land.

He began to shuffle the deck. "The idea is that you wager something of importance. That is what makes it interesting…and worth playing. If you were to wager against me, what would it be?"

She thought for a moment before answering. "I want you to find a more deserving woman. A lady of class to be your countess."

"Strong wager. If I win, you will marry me. That is pretty straight forward, is it not?"

Ivy felt like she was reasoning with a brick wall. "I am the illegitimate daughter of a duke. I was training to be a ballerina in Paris; it will surely cause a scandal when everyone learns of my past. I have nothing to offer you. Will you have that in your bloodline?" she asked, making one last attempt to convince him.

The Earl's eyes darkened. "It matters not. There are pirates, rogues and robbers in my bloodline already."

Despite the rather tense situation, she smiled in genuine amusement. "Under different circumstances, I would ask to hear those stories."

"Another time, I promise." He held out the deck to her and said, "We will each draw a card. If you get the high card, I will stop pursuing you. If I get the high card, then you will marry me. Aces high, of course, in hope of Napoleon's future surrender."

Ivy swallowed, completely ignoring his political witticism.

Dare she let her life hang in the balance over a deck of cards? The Earl's hands were large and steady as they held the deck. Could she marry this man? And if not, would she find anyone more caring in his attentions? The way he gave her gifts was only a small indication of what he would be like as an attentive husband. Her time was running out, both to find a husband and to pick a card. She reached out and chose one, glancing at it.

Queen of Hearts. Few cards were higher.

The Earl quickly pulled his own. "Show them."

She lay down her Queen, unsure if she wanted to win or lose. Not taking his eyes from hers, he placed his card on top of hers.

It was the three of Spades.

Ivy felt despondency bubbling up inside of her. It was foreign and confusing.

"My family has never had much luck with wagers." He rose and stepped out from around the desk and reached for her, helping her stand. His arms encircled her body in his warm, tight embrace.

"What are you doing?" she asked nervously.

He smiled in amusement. "I am going to try and convince you that I would be the best, most caring husband England has to offer you."

She thought he was going to kiss her, but he seemed content just to hold her.

"You do agree I give wonderful gifts? Am I right?"

Ivy smiled. "Yes."

"I enjoy card games, which should signify that I can entertain you…"

Her shoulders shook with laughter as she realized he was not going to accept 'no' for an answer. She sighed as he pulled her closer, and she tucked her head under his chin, enjoying the feeling of being in his arms.

"Is that all it takes to be a good husband?" she asked softly.

He pulled back, forcing her to look up at him. Touching her face, he smiled. "That is not everything."

His firm, sensual lips grazed her cheek and then covered her mouth. Time stopped for her; the Earl's hands cupped her face, his lips eagerly pressing against hers. Her eyes closed as she lost herself to the moment, desire unfurling deep in her belly. When he pulled back, her eyelids fluttered open. He was looking arrogantly pleased.

"Passion is not reason enough to marry," she said quietly as she regained her balance.

"True," he agreed. "Marry me because you think we will have a chance at being truly happy together."

Her eyes glittered with emotion as she reached up to touch his cheek. "Are marriages among the *ton* not usually happy?"

He reached up to grasp her hand in his, and turned his head to kiss her palm. "People usually only tolerate each other. Most dare not ask for more."

Ivy was in turmoil. Her mother accepted what little the Duke offered, but Ivy wanted, and truly needed more. If she was to spend her life with a man, she did not want a relationship like her mother's.

"My mother had so little of the man she loved," Ivy admitted openly. "They had passion, but over the years I watched the light in my mother's eyes dim each time he left her for his other family." She needed him to understand she would be nothing like her mother. She would not accept so little.

"They loved each other, did they not?" he asked.

Love. The word terrified her. Her mother had sacrificed everything because she loved the Duke. It chipped away at her existence, leaving her a hollow shell.

"You do not love me," Ivy stated. "You desire me. You want children with me, perhaps, but love has never entered into your reasons for marriage." She watched as his jaw clenched. "I dare you to deny it."

"I will not speak further of love, Ivy, but you should give me a chance to prove to you that our marriage would be nothing like your mother's relationship with the Duke. I will not cast you aside, or use desire against you. Give me a chance and I shall give you the world."

She stared into his tumultuous and expressive gray eyes, feeling her will bend. Was this the beginning? Would he break her?

"Must I have one without the other? Are all women of my family doomed for such a fate?" She closed her eyes in pain, but heard herself say, "Yes, My Lord. I will marry you."

"Cy," he corrected forcefully.

"Cy," she echoed.

She did not know if she would have a better life than her mother, but she could not marry another man and risk settling for less than what Cy had to offer her. He gave her honesty. Perhaps it would be enough to build a life on.

Once the reality that she was engaged to the Earl of Stanton set in, she began to panic. Ivy had been engaged only a few minutes, and already her thoughts began to spin out of control with worry. It was one thing to wear dresses and to converse at the Duchess's side, but to take her place as a society wife was an entirely different matter.

"Stop panicking. Take a deep breath," he commanded.

"How did you—"

"You got very pale and started shaking. I must say I was hoping my future bride would be overjoyed at the prospect of marrying me. You look in danger of fainting."

She laughed, feeling the tension and worry dissolve.

"That is more like it. Shall we impart the good news to your family?" Cy asked with a tender smile.

When she nodded, he dipped his head again and whispered softly, "Let us seal our engagement with another kiss."

He did not give her time to agree or disagree. He covered her mouth with his, effortlessly molding his lips to hers. Surprising herself, she wrapped her arms around him and kissed him back. Gently, he cupped the back of her neck and she sank into him, loving his hands in her silky tendrils of hair.

He lifted his mouth from hers. "I love your reaction when I touch you," he whispered thickly. "Even now, your face is flushed with passion and your lips are pouty and delectable."

She shivered at his heated words. Cy ran a thumb across Ivy's bottom lip. She inhaled sharply. He placed his hand on her arm and escorted her to the hallway toward the front door. When they arrived out front, the mare snorted in greeting, tossing her elegant head, vying for Ivy's attention.

"Did you ride here without a saddle?" he asked.

"Yes." She fought the urge to squirm. "I received a lecture from Simms and our stable groom already, and they have assured me that my secret is safe with them. Might I ask for the same tact to be employed by you and your servants? The Duchess need not ever know." Her eyes were pleading with him to agree and keep quiet.

He looked down at her beautiful face and replied, "On one condition: you will not ride without a saddle again. Though I am in awe of your skill, my future countess must ride sidesaddle." He said it softly, but with a thread of steel in his voice.

She turned from him, and nodded her head. "You are right… you would be disgraced. And by marrying me I will be disgrace enough."

He reached out a hand to pull her into his arms. "I am thinking of you, Ivy," he said quietly as he stroked her red curls. "I would not want to give the harpies of society any reason to question whether or not you belong with them. And you *do* belong with them. And with me."

He tilted her face back so that she was forced to look at him. His eyes were warm with sincerity and he had a look Ivy was learning to recognize; he wanted to kiss her again. Cy chuckled when she gently pushed him away. If he kissed her, there would be very little chance she would be able to leave any time soon. He muddled her thoughts.

Ivy looked at the mare and said wistfully, "She really is quite beautiful and spirited."

"I wonder if I will be able to deny you anything. I shall let you ride one last time without a saddle. We shall take the long way back to Cavehill land." He squeezed her fingers affectionately and spoke to a footman to see that his horse was readied. Moments later, they were galloping across the rolling landscape, and Ivy could not believe how quickly her life had changed since arriving in England.

When they reached the Cavehill stables, Cy tossed his reins to the waiting stable boy and helped Ivy dismount. He held her for a moment longer than was necessary, and when she looked up at him, she bit her lip, silently pleading for him to kiss her again. He grinned slowly, as if he knew what she wanted.

As he escorted her toward the manor, he whispered into her ear, "I am overjoyed that you want me to kiss you."

She gasped. "*Un diable*!"

He laughed as they walked into the drawing room, finding the Duchess enjoying a cup of tea.

"Hello, Your Grace," Cy greeted.

"Stanton," the Duchess said, inclining her head.

"Where is Willow?" Ivy inquired.

"Painting. Shall I call for her?" the Duchess asked.

When Willow joined them, she turned to Cy and said, "Pleasure to meet you, My Lord."

Cy bowed. "I am glad to finally meet your acquaintance."

"Please, sit," the Duchess remarked.

When they were all seated, Ivy began, "The Earl of Stanton and I…have agreed… that is…" She looked at Cy beseechingly.

"I have asked Ivy to marry me and she has accepted," he said succinctly, giving Ivy a grin and wink.

The Duchess showed very little reaction to the news of her granddaughter's engagement. Willow was not so tightlipped.

"This is wonderful!" Willow looked at Cy and said, "You do know you must give the sister of your intended bride gifts to ensure that she supports the match."

Cy threw his head back and shouted with laughter and said, "I wonder how much this will cost me."

"Ivy loves horses, but if you would like to have a sculpture erected in my honor, that would be perfectly acceptable," Willow said blithely.

"I will have it commissioned at once," Cy teased.

Once they all celebrated with a quick glass of champagne, Cy excused himself to leave. As Ivy saw him out, Willow looked at the Duchess and said, "Are you not happy with the outcome?"

The Duchess's stoic face remained impassive. "Happy? I am actually quite ecstatic."

Willow's mouth quirked into a smile and she joked, "Oh yes, I must have forgotten. That *is* your 'happy' face."

The Duchess did not smile, but Willow swore she saw a glimmer of amusement.

Chapter VI

Hampshire, England, April of 1815

"I thought it would be appropriate to spend a few hours each day with my new fiancée," Cy explained to Ivy the next afternoon when he came to call.

She smiled thoughtfully and asked, "Are you courting me, sir? *After* the betrothal?"

He winked. "I must make sure you have no reason to leave me at the altar."

"Ah," she replied in understanding. "Then by all means, court away."

Cy laughed. "Do you play chess?"

"No."

"Care to learn?" He reached for the bell on the side table and rang for a maid to bring them a chess set. After the maid left, Ivy picked up the ornately carved pieces and began to examine them.

Cy then began to teach her the rudiments of chess. An hour later she had him laughing uproariously when she groaned, "This will take years to master! I am making up my own rules." She then moved her Queen illegally and jumped a few spaces so that her Queen was in front of Cy's King.

"Check mate."

Cy looked at her for a moment and then remarked good-naturedly, "Then I get to make up my own rules, too."

She inclined her head. "Naturally."

He leaned over and brushed his lips against hers. "I want stories. I want to know everything about you. I am ravenous for information."

Warmth settled low in her belly, desire twirling through her. Only Cy had ever made her feel this way, like she had performed a dozen pirouettes in a row. She felt lightheaded, her breathing shallow. His mouth was close to hers, the male scent of him doing dangerous things to her mind.

"Tell me about your life in Paris, your childhood." He reached out to stroke her cheek.

She smiled, enjoying his outward show of affection. She thought for a moment. "I pummeled a boy when I was thirteen years old."

Cy choked on his laughter. "Go on."

"What, no condemnation or shock?"

"Neither. You are a pugnacious hoyden."

"That sounds like an insult."

"On the contrary. I meant it as a compliment. Tell me the story."

Ivy rested her hand on the black rook and began, "I was finishing my last ballet class of the day, and Willow was waiting for me so we could walk home together. I changed, and met her outside, and as we began our trek home she started to cry. Some local boys had been taunting her, you see. They were calling her names like 'bastard' and 'whore child'." She smiled without humor. "Paris claims to be so modern, but apparently it is just a smooth veneer of propriety with a mass of proletarian behavior beneath the surface.

"I left Willow at home, crying in our bedroom. I snuck out, and found the ringleader of the young boys who had been harassing her. They teased and insulted me, but I marched up to the leader and punched him square in the nose."

She made a fist as she remembered that day. Her heart had been pounding with fear and anger, but her steps had never faltered. She had been the avenging angel her sister needed. "My fist hurt for three days, but they never bothered Willow again."

"You are magnificent," he breathed. He reached a hand out and laced his fingers through her curls. As he sought her mouth, she closed her eyes and sighed when his lips covered hers. His tongue swept inside, and she kissed him back, straining closer. Her heart beat rapidly, like a thousand winged creatures taking flight.

He ended the kiss and she growled in frustration. She wanted his warmth, his desire. "Not yet," she murmured audaciously, and then pressed her lips to his for another searing kiss.

"God, you will be the death of me," he gritted out when they finally pulled apart. "You make me want to sweep the chess set off the table, lay you down and slowly lift your skirts." She shivered at the lust in his voice, and he went on, "I want to make you quiver with need and watch your eyes glaze with desire."

"You shock me, sir," she said on a pant.

"We will have honesty between us, Ivy. Never doubt how much I desire you."

"It overwhelms me," she admitted. "But I am not afraid."

"It should," he murmured. "Your innocent candor has the power to sweep away all my noble intentions. I should leave."

She stared at him and asked, "Must you go?"

"It would be dangerous for me to stay. I do not know how much more I can take…" He placed a soft kiss on her forehead and exited the room.

Ivy closed her eyes, touched her lips with her fingertips and shivered. Passion this strong should have terrified her, but for some reason she felt incredibly safe in Cy's arms. When he spoke of what was between them, any resistance she might have felt melted away. Was this how it was between her mother and father? Was this the reason her mother had thrown caution to the wind and accepted what small offerings she was given?

Ivy pursed her lips. Though Cy had promised marriage, he had not promised love. Was she destined, like her mother, to be with a man who could only give her a small piece of himself?

Would that be enough for her?

***

His night was haunted with visions of Ivy. He dreamed of her silken, ivory skin, his body covering hers as she writhed beneath his as he made her soar. When he awoke, he was left shaken and short of breath. He was strung tighter than a bow.

He had never wanted a woman the way he wanted Ivy. He yearned to possess her as she possessed him; to know that sleep could not claim her because she was restless from wanting. Every time he kissed her, he lost more control, needing her touch, needing to feel her tentative, innocent hands journey over his smoldering body. When she had taken control and kissed him, he thought he would die of lust.

Gritting his teeth in distress, he threw off the covers and put on a dressing robe. He made his way downstairs to the library, poured himself a liberal amount of brandy and settled down to wait for dawn, knowing it would not ease his torment.

***

Her afternoon with Cy in the library left her shaken. She could not believe her own shamelessness, or Cy's deliciously naughty words to her. It left her breathless and mortified that she had spurned him on, but helpless to stop it. She did not think young women were at all eager for this sort of attention. It only proved to her that she was, indeed, not a lady.

That night, Ivy pleaded to have a headache so she could be excused from dinner. She went to bed early, but sleep eluded her. Watching the dawn's rays creep through the blue curtains, she finally decided to rise. She had not slept much, and there was no point lingering in bed. She did not ring for a maid but chose instead to dress herself in a dark purple riding habit. She walked to the stables and apologized to the sleepy stable boy, who promptly saddled the lively mare Cy had given her. She mounted the horse and rode off at a breakneck pace. She took in deep breaths, hoping to dispel the tension boiling with in her.

Ballet used to soothe her in every way, but now she turned to riding. In the past, she had only enjoyed riding moderately but now found great pleasure in it. *When had the change come?* she wondered.

As she looped around the countryside, she slowed her mare and headed back towards her grandmother's property. She decided it was best not to question life further, and declared to be more carefree and willing to accept the things that were happening to her, for she was unable to change or stop them.

When she arrived back to the manor, she had an early breakfast alone and then went upstairs for a nap. Ivy awoke in early afternoon, feeling quite restored.

A maid bustled into her room and said, "Miss Ivy! Thank goodness you are finally awake! The Earl of Stanton is downstairs!"

Desperately wanting a bath, she replied, "Please tell him I will be down shortly."

'Shortly' turned into an hour. She found Cy in the drawing room playing chess with Willow, who seemed to be a much better student than Ivy. He rose when she entered and reached for her hand. She noticed the shadows beneath his eyes and wondered about them.

"Forgive me for making you wait," she said.

Cy kissed her hand. "Not at all. Your sister was indulging me in a game of chess."

He smiled at Willow, who replied, "I am quite intrigued with this game now."

Ivy shook her head. "Then perhaps you should help me the next time I play against the Earl. I have no skill for the game and will need every bit of help."

They all laughed.

"Good to see you, My Lord," Willow said with a curtsy just before she threw her sister a swift look and left the room. The door closed, and Cy and Ivy were alone.

"How did you sleep?"

Ivy grinned sheepishly. "I saw the dawn, then went for an early morning ride, came home and then promptly took a nap. And you?"

He tugged on her hand and kissed her palm. "I, too, saw the dawn. Come, I have a picnic planned for us."

"A picnic?" she asked.

He grinned. "I am appealing to your sense of adventure."

On their way out, a smiling maid handed them a basket. Cy took Ivy's hand in his and led her outside into the sunny day. As they made their way through open fields, Ivy noticed the new blooms of spring. A plethora of purple, pink and blue flowers scattered their path, their fragrance tickling her nose.

Cy escorted her to the top of a hill around a bend, just out of view of any possible passersby. He spread out a plaid blanket that was in the basket and made sure she was settled before he took a seat next to her. She made a grab for the basket and began to unpack it. Delighted, she pulled out cold chicken, rolls and dried fruit. They sat together quietly and exchanged thoughtful looks as they ate.

Once they were finished eating, Cy took out a deck of cards and grinned, "Ready for a game?"

Ivy feigned wariness. "Oh no, the last time I played cards with you I managed to get myself engaged. Who knows what could happen next…"

"The worst has already happened," Cy joked. "We will not be wagering today."

"Every moment I spend with you, I find myself more and more comfortable in your presence," he admitted.

She blushed at his brash statement. "I never thought such a simple afternoon could be so enjoyable."

Looking at Cy, she noticed the admiring look on his face. She swallowed as she stared at his sensual mouth. He reached for her, his arms stealing around her body.

"Ivy," he breathed as his mouth moved dangerously close to her supple, pink lips.

As if of their own volition, her hands roamed up his strong chest, and her fingers settled into the hair at the base of his neck and pressed her lips to his.

She opened her mouth, letting his tongue sweep in and entwine with hers. Ivy did not know if the resulting sounds of pleasure were hers or Cy's; it did not matter. She wanted him desperately, and she clung to him fiercely. He tilted her head to the side and trailed his lips down her flushed cheek, over her feminine jawline and down the side of her tender nape. When his hand found her breast, she arched against him and gave in to the tumultuous pleasure. She was lustful and deprived and she did not care.

Cy loomed over her as he gently positioned her on the blanket. The dying afternoon sunlight was behind him, bathing him in an ethereal glow. She reached up to touch his cheek, and slid her hand down to his chest again so that she felt his rapid heartbeat.

"May I?" he asked huskily even as his fingers went to the small buttons of her riding habit.

Unable to form a response, she nodded, wanting his warm hands on her sensitive flesh.

He sighed as he exposed her creamy skin. Cy's head, covered in immaculate dark hair, bent over her chest as he kissed her collarbone and moved lower. With a few deft movements, he liberated her breasts from her bodice. For a long moment, he simply stared. His gaze was reverent and hungry.

"They are perfect," he said of her round, creamy breasts with dainty pink nipples. "Better than my dream."

"Dream?" Ivy asked, her voice breathy with banked longing.

He did not answer, but his smile was slow, hot, and it inflamed her. He reached out to gently tease her nipple. It puckered. Without warning Cy did something Ivy never expected; he took one ripe bud into his mouth and sucked.

She gasped in unexpected pleasure as he continued to assault her virtuous flesh. When she thought she would die of sweet torment, he moved to the other mound and paid it lavish attention. She arched against him, realizing her body recognized the ancient call of desire.

"So beautiful," he said huskily. His eyes seemed almost black with desire, and he smiled gently. He moved even lower as he slowly spread her shapely legs and hiked up her skirts.

Ivy weakly attempted to make him stop, her mind knowing she should, but her body betrayed her. "Cy…" she breathed. She was oblivious to everything except the quaking hunger within her.

"It is all right, love."

He gazed at her curly red knoll that gently shielded her most intimate prize. Touching her with one finger, he let out a male grunt of satisfaction. "You are so wet," he rasped. "Slick with desire for me."

She threw her head back in ecstasy, uncaring that her body was bared to him. And then he did something so intimate, so incredible, Ivy thought she would burst. Cy put his mouth on her delicate, rosy core and began to lick her honeyed folds. He sucked on her throbbing bud as she thrashed from all-consuming pleasure. A warm fire started to burn low in her belly, and its glow spread. Cy tongued her faster and faster, and when she could take no more, she buckled and nearly screamed, colliding with swells of pleasure that washed over her.

"Dear God," she whispered, refusing to open her eyes.

When she finally did, Cy was smiling, looking like he wanted to pleasure her again. The way she felt, she was inclined to let him. He touched her lightly and she trembled. She was ready for more, and Cy eased a finger into her tight sheath, working his finger slowly. Instinctively, Ivy opened her legs farther, taking him in deeper. He inserted another finger and her damp heat enclosed him as Ivy erupted in passion for the second time. Gently, he disengaged himself and pulled her skirts lower, giving her a moment regain her breath.

"Did you enjoy that, love?" he asked.

She turned liquid green eyes to his face and smiled slightly. "I think I did," she admitted.

He chuckled. "It gets much better, too. Trust me."

"When?" She could not stop herself from asking. She wanted him to hold her and lean her head against his chest.

"When we are married," he promised. "I will love you all night long, until the sun comes up."

Ivy swallowed, her mouth suddenly dry. She wanted it now, she realized, trembling in need.

Cy's gaze was hungry and he playfully admonished, "Stop looking at me that way, or I might forget all my good intentions to wait."

***

Over the next week, Cy rarely came to call. He kept his distance, and it left Ivy bereft and confused. Blushing at the memory of their picnic, she thought perhaps he was ashamed of her behavior. She had been wanton and needy and she was deeply embarrassed by her actions.

Even when Cy did come to see her, his visits were brief. Was he losing interest? Did he no longer want her?

Ivy became a rolling mass of conflicting feelings and anxiety. She had more in common with her mother than she realized. She needed to remember her pride and dignity. She would not make the mistake again of behaving like a shameless hussy in his presence.

If her fiancé could remain detached, so could she.

Chapter VII

Hampshire, England, May of 1815

Ivy stood in front of the mirror barely recognizing the vision that stared back at her. Her curls were pinned up, a rope of pearls peeking out through her shining red tresses. The dress she wore was pale ivory and accentuated her small waist and graceful neck.

There was a knock on the door and a moment later, Willow entered wearing a white gown with gold chains woven through her blonde hair.

"You look beautiful," Willow said as she took Ivy's hand and squeezed it.

"So do you. Can you believe we are here at this moment? I am wearing a dress that costs more than rent on our flat in Paris."

Willow shook her head. "One minute we were on a path destined for the stage, and the next we are in England about to attend a ball that informally presents us to society."

"Life has some interesting twists," Ivy said. "I am glad you are here with me, Willow."

They walked down the stairs and into the drawing room where the Duchess was waiting for them. There was a knock, and a footman in his formalwear of green and gold livery entered.

"All the guests have arrived, Your Grace. They are in the ballroom."

"Thank you, Simms," the Duchess said. "I would like a moment with my granddaughters."

Simms retreated and the Duchess faced Ivy and Willow. Both look startled, since the woman had never referred to them as family before. Perhaps she was finally accepting them.

She nodded in quick approval at their appearances. "Remember, this is not your entrance to high society. You are only meeting a small group of close friends and acquaintances, but it is still good practice," she nearly barked. "And you may call me 'grandmother.'"

A feather or a stiff breeze could have knocked the girls over, so in shock by the Duchess's request. Ivy and Willow looked at each other in astonishment, but then proceeded to follow the Duchess.

When the three of them entered the exquisitely decorated ballroom, the guests stopped in mid-conversation and a full twenty seconds passed before a striking woman near thirty, approached them. The silence of the room was broken and everyone began speaking again.

"May I introduce the Countess of Langley," the Duchess said. "My granddaughters, Miss Ivy and Miss Willow Sinclair."

"It is a pleasure to meet you. Thank you for coming," Ivy said with a sincere smile and a curtsy.

"We have known the Duchess a long time and we would not have missed this for the world. My husband is around here somewhere, and he will be delighted to meet you both as well."

As Willow struck up a conversation with the lovely woman, Ivy's eyes wandered around the room, and rested on the center of the crowd. As it parted, Cy walked towards her, dressed in black evening attire.

He looked polished and masculine. A shorter, attractive man with brown hair was by his side.

Her breath hitched, taking in Cy's handsome form. She could not believe she was engaged to him, but at once remembered the pledge she had made to herself a week ago. Ivy would not let a man be the source of her happiness. She vowed to remain cool and aloof.

***

When Cy first saw Ivy across the ballroom, it had been a punch to his gut. She was always beautiful, but tonight, seeing her in formalwear, he had a glimpse of how she would look as his countess. For the rest of their lives, she would wear gorgeous ball gowns and his gifts of jewels would twinkle at her ears and throat. He was so incredibly proud of her and the regal picture she presented.

"Dear God! That cannot be your fiancée!" the Count of Langley said. Cy's friend appreciatively took in Ivy's red locks, fair face and sensual physique as they both strode towards her.

Cy glared at Langley's blatant perusal of Ivy's features. "Quiet please, Langley. I told you she was my fiancée in confidence. It has not been announced yet."

"Dear God, man, announce it! It will keep all the young bucks away from her. Stake your claim." As they approached the group of women, the Count joined his wife's side, and Cy moved close to Ivy.

"Would you like something to drink?" Cy asked Ivy, leaning over to whisper in her ear.

He saw her stiffen. He placed her hand on his sleeve and guided her through the crowd of guests, who peered at them in wonder. He wanted a moment alone with her away from the ears of her family.

The last two weeks had been sheer torture for him. Maintaining his distance had been the only way to keep himself from taking her virtue. Even now, he wanted to trail a finger down the line of her elegant, swanlike neck and watch her shiver in pleasure. He wanted to plunge his hands into her bodice, plunder her mouth, and hear her greedy cries of passion.

Cy handed her a glass of champagne from a passing servant and took his own. Over the rim of his flute, he watched Ivy's hands shake as she lifted her glass to her plump, inviting lips. He knew he was watching her with a predatory stillness that went beyond a simple escort, but he felt possessive. He did not care who noticed or who talked.

"Are you enjoying the ball?" she asked.

It was the first thing she had said to him that evening and it sounded breathless. Dare he think she was as affected by him as he was by her?

"I am enjoying watching you," he said honestly. He was glad to note his comment made her cheeks bloom with warmth. "I would like to apologize for my absence the last couple of weeks. I thought it wise after our time together at the picnic."

Ivy would not meet his eyes, but he noticed her heightened color had not faded.

"Do you regret it, then?" she asked softly.

Cy wanted to curse. So wrapped up in his own desires, he did not think how Ivy would take his negligence. Reaching out to grasp her chin, he slowly forced her to look him directly in the eyes.

"Regret is not the word I would choose." He pitched his voice low so as not to be overheard. "I want to do it again."

"You do?" Ivy asked, her eyes widening in shock and wonder.

He nodded. "So much in fact, that the only way I knew to stop myself was to keep away from you."

"Then, you do not find me…brazen?" Her cheeks flushed again.

Leaning over he whispered in her ear, "I find you *very* brazen, but I would not have you any other way." On the contrary, he was thinking about having her every which way.

Ivy gave a long shuddering sigh. "You still want to marry me?"

"Very much."

Ivy turned her attention to Willow who was conversing with the Count and Countess of Langley. "I hope my sister finds someone as charming and genuine as you," she said.

"What a nice compliment."

"It is true. I do believe my sister will have all the success. She will have dozens of suitors falling at her feet."

"Does part of you yearn to have other suitors at your feet?"

She shook her head and gazed into his warm, gray eyes. "I am quite content with my present situation, and the prospect of my future."

"I am glad to hear it." He took a step closer so that his jacket touched the front of her dress.

With the tines of a fork on a heavy crystal glass, an immaculately dressed footman announced to all that dinner was served, and the spell between the two was broken.

Talking with Ivy was similar to drinking an entire bottle of champagne, Cy thought; his tongue loosened and he easily forgot the world around him.

He would have to marry her, and soon.

***

Dinner was an intimate yet extravagant affair. The Duchess was known for her immaculate taste, and that night it showed. Red silk tablecloths graced the long dinner table and gold candelabras held dripping wax candles that bathed the dining room in delicate light. Plates and silverware were all perfectly placed, and no object in the room was anything other than absolutely perfect.

Ivy sat across the table from Cy, whose gray eyes seemed to smolder when he looked at her. He seemed to barely register the exquisite taste of his lamb shank; instead his focus was entirely on her. Her hand shook when she lifted her wine glass, and she wondered how she was going to make it to dessert. All she wanted were Cy's lips on hers, especially after he admitted to liking her forward behavior.

When it was time for the gentlemen to leave the table and enjoy after dinner drinks and cigars, the Duchess suggested the ladies retire to a separate salon so they might converse more comfortably. Excusing herself, Ivy sought the spacious, dimly lit water closet. Two women entered without noticing Ivy, and just as she was about to make her presence known, they started talking about Cy. Intrigued, she kept to the shadows, eager to hear what they were saying.

"Did you see how he was looking at Miss Sinclair? He could not tear his eyes away from her."

"I know! What do you suppose Miss Fitzgerald will do when she hears about this?"

"Who knows?" the first woman asked. "I heard the Earl was just about to finalize his engagement plans with her father, and now here he is with Miss Sinclair. He is being rather possessive, standing close to her and never leaving her side."

Her friend sighed. "The way the Earl was gazing at Miss Sinclair, I highly doubt Miss Fitzgerald will be the next Countess of Stanton."

"She should not have alluded to it until the betrothal was settled."

"The Earl certainly likes women of all types. I once saw him with his tall, brunette mistress outside the millinery's shop."

Their voices died out as they left the water closet, still entirely unaware that Ivy had heard their entire exchange. Ivy shook with anger from the news as she looked into the mirror and fixed an errant curl. *Could it be true?* Had Cy been engaged to this Miss Fitzgerald? Was a wife so interchangeable that he had seen Ivy and simply decided he wanted her instead? How dare he! And to hear about his *mistress*!

It was a painful subject for Ivy. Their mother had been a mistress to their father, and Ivy and Willow were the result of that relationship. Was a woman doomed to being either the mother of his heir, or his woman of passion? Were they never one in the same?

She returned to the drawing room and somehow managed to converse politely with the other occupants, but all the while she wished she was upstairs alone in her room so she could think about all that she had heard. At the end of the evening, the Duchess and Willow were busy escorting their guests to the door and Ivy was momentarily left alone with Cy.

"That was a delightful evening," Cy remarked, his eyes roving over her face. "Would you like to go riding tomorrow afternoon?"

"No, thank you," she dismissed. "I promised Willow I would go shopping with her."

He paused a moment. "Ivy," he said softly. "What is the matter? I thought we had settled everything between us."

Did he call Miss Fitzgerald by her first name, too? she thought waspishly.

Ivy looked at him directly and smiled sweetly. "Have a wonderful night, My Lord. Thank you for coming."

She turned on her heel and walked away.

***

The next morning, the Duchess buttered a scone as she said, "After last night, I have no qualms that with a few more weeks of lessons, you both will be completely ready to take your places in society. I am very proud of the both of you."

"Thank you," Willow said in obvious surprise by the praise. "It was a lovely ball. Your friends and neighbors were delightful and very accepting of us."

Ivy said nothing as she continued to stare at her plate of food. She pushed it around with her fork, but did not have much of an appetite.

"What did you think, Ivy?" the Duchess asked. "Did you enjoy yourself?"

"How would she know? She was too busy looking into the Earl of Stanton's eyes," Willow teased.

The Duchess laughed, shocking both Ivy and Willow, who looked at the woman like she had grown two heads. She was in rare spirits today. "I knew I was right introducing the two of you."

Ivy was spared from answering when Simms came into the dining room and announced that Ivy had a visitor.

"Who is it?" Ivy asked.

"The Earl of Stanton, Miss Ivy."

Ivy's face flushed with anger, but she composed herself into a portrait of politeness. Sweeping into the salon, she held her chin high, her molten waves cascading down her back.

Cy turned and smiled. "Good morning. You look lovely."

"Thank you," she replied tightly. "What are you doing here?"

He frowned in discernable confusion. "Paying a morning call. I thought that was obvious," he said sarcastically.

She shot him a condescending look. "I thought *I* had made it clear that I was occupied today."

A flash of annoyance crossed Cy's strong face, and then, with sardonic amusement he said, "All right, Ivy. Apparently I have done something to upset you. Will you tell me what it is so I can apologize and buy you something to atone for being such a beast?"

Heat suffused her face. "What makes you think you did anything?" she challenged. "And what makes you think you can buy my affection?"

He stalked towards her in two long strides and grasped her by the arms. She struggled to shake him off, but his hands were like iron shackles. Angry, green eyes clashed with calm, curious gray ones.

"What did I do, Ivy?" he asked softly, his warm breath near her mouth.

"Nothing," she denied nervously.

His head descended towards hers and he whispered, "I do not believe you."

His mouth closed over hers and his lips fit as if they were made for her mouth alone. Cy's hands moved from her arms to her back, drawing her closer to his hard body. She tried to remain uninvolved, but she could not. Anger and lust collided, leaving her body feeling tight, like her skin was stretched too thin. He lifted his head and gazed into her eyes and brushed his thumbs over her cheeks.

"Am I forgiven?"

"There is nothing to forgive. If you will excuse me, I have some letters to write."

She extricated herself from his arms and left the room. She was proud of herself that she had managed to sound aloof, but ashamed that she had kissed him back. She realized, in a battle against her desire for Cy, she would most definitely lose.

***

"The Earl of Stanton is in the drawing room with Grandmother. She requests your presence immediately," Willow said from the doorway of Ivy's bedroom.

"Why?" Ivy asked, not getting up off her bed.

"Wedding preparations, I imagine. I will be practicing the pianoforte if you need me. If you discuss the color of my dress, remember I look terrible in puce."

Willow's jest did not make Ivy smile. Reluctantly and petulantly, Ivy trekked to the drawing room. It had been two days since she had stormed out on Cy, and during that time of silence, she had spent most of her time riding. She refused to answer any questions posed to her by her grandmother or sister as to what was wrong. Now, however, she would be forced to face Cy. She was not ready for a confrontation, for she always seemed to lose her train of thought in his presence. He had been engaged to another woman before her; she could not forget that fact.

Ivy entered the drawing room and her gaze found Cy's, who was sitting calmly in the corner. After Ivy was settled with a cup of tea, the Duchess turned the conversation to wedding plans.

"Stanton and I agree that it is best for a quick engagement. After all, there is no reason for a long one."

Ivy raised an elegant red brow and said, "No? On the contrary, I thought a long engagement would be just the thing. It might give the Earl some time to decide if I am the right woman for him."

Clearly startled, the Duchess looked at Cy who was watching Ivy with a steadfast gaze. "I have already decided that you are the right woman for me, Ivy," Cy said softly.

"Oh? What about Miss Emily Fitzgerald?"

"What about Miss Fitzgerald?" he answered vaguely.

"At the ball, I heard a rumor that you were about to finalize a betrothal agreement with her father just before we met. I also learned of your mistress, and apparently she is quite beautiful."

"Ivy!" the Duchess lashed out. "You do *not* speak of a man's paramour in mixed company!"

Ivy looked coldly at her grandmother and said, "I am the child of such a relationship." She then turned her challenging stare to Cy and taunted, "Or have you forgotten, My Lord?"

"Your Grace," Cy said through a clenched jaw, "will you excuse us for one moment? It seems Ivy and I need to settle a dispute."

The Duchess stood and left the tension filled room.

Ivy glared at Cy, furious that he appeared unruffled. Just once she would like to see him lose control, as he had made her lose control countless times in his arms. It was not fair!

"Why should it bother you that I was engaged to Miss Fitzgerald?" he asked steadily.

She could not believe it. She expected denial, or sputtering to conceal his past, but not open admittance. "You do not even deny it?"

"What would be the point? You clearly have judged and condemned me already for it. Lying does no good."

"It is not the engagement I am concerned about but the timing," she said through gritted teeth.

That was not entirely true. The idea that Cy had been engaged to another woman infuriated her. Did he take liberties with her too? Did he stroke her body, making it hum like a taut string? Had he kissed Miss Fitzgerald senseless?

He rose and strode closer to her. Taking her hand, he pulled her up into his arms.

Ivy's mood was dark and stormy as she asked, "Did you kiss her? Touch her?"

"No," he said softly.

"I desperately want to believe you."

"Have I ever done anything to make you not trust me? Honesty, remember?" Cy gently framed her face in his hands and said, "You are perfect for me, Ivy. Miss Fitzgerald does not compare to your beauty, your passion, your fire."

"And…your mistress?" she asked hesitantly.

He sighed. "I do not currently have a mistress."

"Currently?" she asked irritably.

The man had the nerve to smile. "I have not had one for years."

"Will you have one after we are married?"

"Boldness becomes you," he murmured.

"Answer me," she demanded.

"I only want a wife."

"Truly?" she asked, the tension around her heart easing.

"Truly," he repeated as his lips descended towards hers.

She reached up to meet him, and her arms slowly intertwined around his neck as she sought solace in his embrace. Cy's hands wove through her curls and kept her lips pressed firmly against his. His tongue swept through her mouth, and her knees buckled with desire. She leaned into him, wanting to get closer.

Abruptly, he grasped her arms and gently pushed her away from him. He was breathing hard and Ivy was short of breath, too. Her lips tingled, and she felt lightheaded with lust.

"Yes," Cy rasped. "A short engagement is necessary. How do you feel about marrying in four months?"

She looked at him and said, "Yes. If you can wait that long."

He grinned. "Three months it is."

Chapter VIII

Hampshire, England

Ivy woke up early before most of the house was awake. She passed sleepy chambermaids and footmen as she made her way to the kitchen. She took bread, cheese and an apple for her breakfast and was out the back door before the sun even poked its head over the hills. She walked to the small, flat clearing she had discovered in the first few days at her grandmother's home.

As the sun rose and began to warm everything it touched, she stripped off her wool cloak. Standing in nothing but her makeshift ballet attire, she took a deep breath and went through the repetitive steps to loosen her muscles, staying limber so they would not cramp.

She had continued to condition her body each day, just as she had done every morning since she was seven years old. Since she had come to England, her life had taken on new challenges, but she missed the rigors of ballet. It was the one thing from her old life she did not want to forget, and she would not shame her mother's memory by choosing to ignore such a profound part of herself.

When she was finished her routine, she breathed in deeply and enjoyed the scent of fresh air among the trees. She sat down on a rock, and ate the small breakfast she had packed. The sun had moved behind the clouds, causing a slight chill; she wrapped her cloak around her. By the time she was finished eating, she was still not ready to go back to the house, enjoying her solitude far too much. She decided to take a walk with no particular direction in mind. Ballet had invigorated her and she had energy to spare as she leisurely strolled across the land.

The storm came out of nowhere.

As the rain began to fall, she realized she was closer to Cy's estate than she was to her grandmother's. She ran toward his home, but not before the sky opened up and unleashed a torrential downpour. She was drenched, shivering and muddy by the time she knocked on the front door.

The butler instantly ushered her inside. "Miss Ivy!" he exclaimed.

Ivy was dripping on the wood floor as the butler called out orders to servants for a hot bath. Maids and footmen bustled around her with towels, trying to soak up the water on the floor around her.

"What in thunder…" Cy popped his head out of the study and in surprise said, "Ivy! What are you doing here?"

She tried to smile, but sneezed instead, clutching a towel to the tip of her nose. "I am sorry to intrude. I was out for a walk, and I got caught in the storm," she explained.

He raised his eyebrows. "You are not intruding. You came here?"

"It was closer." She sneezed again.

Cy took her hand and led her up the stairs. "And here I thought it was because you actually wanted to see me."

She smiled. "Arrogance becomes you."

He laughed as he opened the door to an expansive guest room. It was decorated in gold and blue brocade, and had its own washroom.

A maid bustled in and said, “I will have a bath ready for you soon, Miss Sinclair.”

“Thank you,” Ivy said, and then turned to Cy. “Will you send a note to my grandmother?”

“She does not know you are here?”

Ivy looked chagrined. “I escaped early this morning. I wanted time by myself.”

He raised his eyebrows and asked, “What do you do when you are alone?”

“I practice,” she said. “Ballet. Please do not tell her what I was doing. She thinks I have given it up.”

“She will not hear it from me,” he promised. “I will send a note to your grandmother immediately so she will not worry.”

“Thank you. Do not let me keep you from your day.”

“I was only reading investment papers. Very boring documents. Your presence is a welcome excuse to stop.” He looked at her. “I will request that your sister come and keep you company. She can bring you a change of clothes.”

“That is not necessary,” Ivy protested.

“Nonsense. I will also summon a doctor. No use fighting me. I am your fiancé and it is my duty to see to your welfare.”

She inclined her head and smiled. “So be it, My Lord.”

***

Cy escorted Willow into his study and said, "Your sister is upstairs having a bath and then she is being put to bed. I know she will be glad to see you. Before you tend to her, I wanted to ask your opinion about the wedding present I am planning on giving her." Willow raised her eyebrows as he went on, "Did you know your sister still practices ballet?"

Willow laughed and nodded. "Of course. She refuses to stop."

Cy cleared his throat. "I would like to construct a studio for her use. A real ballet studio, complete with mirrors and bars."

Willow clasped her hands together in excitement. "I think that would be a perfect gift!"

After tea, he took Willow upstairs, knocked on the door and the maid answered.

"This is Miss Sinclair, Miss Ivy's sister. How is she?"

The maid was standing in Willow's way, preventing her from entering and before the maid could reply, Ivy's muffled voice came through the door. "Is that the arrogant, tyrannical earl? Tell that overbearing man I refuse to stay in bed. I am *fine*!"

Cy pushed past the maid and opened the door widely, revealing Willow.

"I will decide if you are well," he said in an intractable tone. "Now, stay in bed and keep warm. Put another hot brick at her feet," he commanded to the attentive maid.

Ivy glared at him, and then smiled at her sister. "Willow! I am glad you are here."

Willow chuckled. "You should thank your overbearing fiancé. He did send for me."

Ivy looked sheepish.

"I will leave you two ladies, as I have some work that requires my attention." He went to find his butler and demanded, "Have you sent for the doctor?"

Jamison nodded and replied, "Of course, My Lord. He is tending to some of his other patients but will come when he is able."

An hour later, peals of laughter could be heard from the upstairs bedroom. The girls sounded like they were in fine spirits, and Cy wondered if he had been too concerned about Ivy's health. He sighed and pushed away the investment papers. He was unlikely to get anything accomplished with the red-haired siren in his house, so he went up the stairs and poked his head into the guest bedroom.

"Sounds like a lot of fun is happening up here," he replied mock-sternly.

Ivy shook her head. "No fun at all. Willow has been beating me at cards all afternoon. I have to redeem myself. Especially if you will not let me out of bed."

He chose to ignore her pointed comment, pulled up a chair and gathered the cards. "I have a game I would like to teach you both," he said.

"What game would that be?" Willow asked eagerly.

"Poker."

"Poker?" Willow asked. "I have not heard of poker."

Cy grinned. "It is quite new. A good friend that has traveled to America taught me. It is a gentleman's wagering game, and I intend to teach it to the both of you."

"You wish me to learn unladylike hobbies?" Willow asked, pretending to be scandalized.

"As your future brother-in-law, it is my duty to make sure you are prepared for all aspects of society."

Willow laughed.

Cy looked at Ivy and said, "If I recall, you are a fan of wagering, are you not?"

Willow looked quizzically at Ivy, whose flushed cheeks bloomed even more.

Ivy has not divulged the story of my proposal, he realized.

Two hours later, the cards were put away. "It is time for you to rest," Cy commanded.

Ivy's eyes were closing of their own free will as she placed her head on the pillow. "All right," she murmured.

"Sleep well, Ivy," Willow said softly.

Cy leaned over and pressed a kiss to Ivy's forehead. It was warm and he thought she might be feverish.

"I shall keep her here until she is well," he stated as he escorted Willow to the carriage.

Willow raised an eyebrow. "You are most solicitous, sir. I am glad my sister has someone who cares for her well being."

The doctor still had not arrived by dinnertime and Cy's concern grew even as he tried to keep his attention on his investment papers. He dozed off in his study, but at two in the morning his valet roused him awake. Ivy was having a fitful night of sleep; she had a fever and was thrashing around in bed and mumbling.

He went to her immediately, dismissing the attentive chambermaid and thanking her for sitting with Ivy and sponging her forehead to keep her cool. It was a chore Cy intended to take over himself.

Just before dawn the doctor arrived and entered the room. “I am sorry I could not come sooner,” Dr. Cannon, a portly man with bushy eyebrows said. “A woman decided to give birth in the early hours of the morning, and I left only when I could be assured she and the child were safe.”

Cy nodded his head. “Thank you for coming.” He rubbed a hand over his tired and unshaved face. “Ivy got caught in a rainstorm. I made her stay here to make sure she was well, and now I am glad I was so overprotective. She caught a fever last night.”

“Let me take a look,” Dr. Cannon said as he pressed his head against her chest to listen to her lungs. When the doctor was finished examining Ivy and was finally satisfied, he nodded and said, “Nothing to be alarmed about. Just a mild chest cold. I doubt any fluid will fill her lungs. Keep her warm, and when she wakes feed her hot broth. She will be right as rain in a few days.”

“Thank you,” Cy said, and then escorted the doctor downstairs. “I will have some refreshment sent to the drawing room for you to enjoy before you leave. If you will excuse me, I will go back and sit with her.” If the doctor thought Cy’s concern was anything out of the ordinary, he wisely did not comment on it.

When Cy reentered Ivy’s bedroom, he was relieved to find her sleeping soundly. He settled down in the chair next to the bed and fell asleep.

***

Ivy woke to late morning sun filtering through the blue drapes. Her head felt heavy, but she managed to sit up. She inhaled sharply when she saw Cy asleep in the chair next to the bed. She examined him for a moment; his shirtsleeves were rolled up, and his chin was dark with stubble. He was relaxed in sleep; in a way he never looked when he was awake. He was always so assured and in control then, and she liked that about him, but this was different. It was as if she had a glimpse of him at his most vulnerable.

She wanted a glass of water, but when she attempted to get up she became dizzy, and had to grip the bed to keep from falling.

"What are you doing?" a sleepy male voice admonished.

Ivy's vision cleared as Cy came to her, helping settle her back into bed. His dark hair was mussed and she wished she had the energy to stroke it away from his face.

"Water, please," she said, and then closed her eyes. Cy handed her a glass, and sat down on the bed next to her. When she had her fill, she leaned back and said, "Thank you. Have you been here all night?"

He nodded. "You had a rough sleep and a high fever."

"That would explain the odd dreams," she said.

"Dreams?" Cy asked with raised eyebrows.

Ivy nodded. "Shadows of demons, and a lot of red…"

"Fever dreams," Cy concluded. "The doctor came to see you. He does not seem at all concerned. You should be well in a few days. Are you feeling any better?"

"A bit. I felt fine yesterday afternoon, and then right after we played cards I began to feel ill."

Cy stood up. "I will have some hot broth sent up to you. You should drink as much as you can. Doctor's orders…and mine, too."

"Cy…" she said when his hand was on the doorknob. "Thank you for your kindness and generosity."

He came back to her and kissed her forehead. "It is my duty to see to your welfare. Rest. I will visit you later."

While she recovered, her sister came to visit, and Cy spent a good amount of his time with Ivy. Three days later, Ivy was well enough to travel home. A part of her wanted to stay with him, but she realized she would get her wish soon enough.

"Do not get caught in any more rainstorms," the Duchess admonished when Ivy came home.

Cy was standing by her side and replied, "On the contrary, she should get caught in them much more often. It was a true pleasure to be able to take care of her."

Ivy threw him a look. "You refused to let me move about! One would think I was a bedridden invalid."

"It was my right as your fiancé," Cy said high-handedly. "Besides, it got you out of your lessons for three days!"

Ivy laughed. "In that case, I should be kissing the ground you walk on!"

***

The announcement of the engagement between the Earl of Stanton and Miss Ivy Sinclair hit *The Times*, one of England's most prestigious newspapers, and swept through the ranks of nobility like wildfire.

Ivy's status soared. Invitations began to flood the Cavehill country home, arriving in overwhelming amounts from almost every member of high society.

"Very few people know me! How can they want me to come to their soirées?" Ivy asked, completely perplexed.

The Duchess smiled with amusement. "They want to see the woman who snatched up one of the most sought after bachelors who has avoided marriage for years."

Ivy looked at Willow who laughed gleefully and said, "They want to judge you, Ivy."

"She is right," the Duchess agreed. "Though our neighbors adored you and Willow both, there will be those in London that think you are nothing more than impostors."

"Lovely," Ivy said sarcastically. She touched a thick cream envelope. "This one is from Lady Dashwell."

The Duchess smiled joyfully. "You have been officially invited to the Greek Ball. Marvelous!"

"What is the Greek Ball?" Willow asked.

"Every year in late June, Lord and Lady Dashwell throw a Greek Ball. Everyone dresses in

Greek fashion, dines on Greek dishes, and the ballroom looks like an ancient Greek Temple. It is simply splendid. The night of the ball will be your official entrance into society just as I had planned."

Ivy stifled a groan. "Does this mean a new gown?"

"It does, indeed," the Duchess said. "Is the Earl of Stanton coming for dinner this evening?"

Ivy nodded. "Yes, he wants to ensure that I have fully recovered from my cold."

"Perfect. Undoubtedly he has received an invitation to the Greek Ball as well, and will be amenable to joining us."

Ivy felt a curl of pleasure envelope her. The idea of arriving on Cy's arm to her first extravagant ball filled her with a sense of longing. It would be her chance to show Cy and the rest of society that he had not made a mistake by asking for her hand in marriage.

Dinner that evening was a quiet and intimate affair, and noticeably more relaxed than usual. The Duchess was in unusually good spirits, and seemed to have unbent a great deal since the girls first arrived.

"Of course I will be escorting Ivy to the Greek Ball," Cy said, and then smiled at Ivy tenderly. "I have also asked the Count and Countess of Langley to join us that evening."

The Duchess nodded. "Excellent idea. It will be better for us to make a splash."

Willow laughed. "*And*, Ivy will have support in numbers if we show up as a brood."

After dinner was over and Cy had finished a glass of brandy, Ivy escorted him to the door. Willow and the Duchess were still in the drawing room finishing their evening tea, affording Cy and Ivy some privacy.

"I will be leaving for London in a few days. I have some business matters that need my attention," Cy said. "When will you be coming to London with your grandmother and sister?"

"In two weeks. She would like Willow and I to settle in before the rigors of the Season start, and we have to prepare for the Greek Ball, of course."

He smiled. "She is wise. May I invite you and your family to dinner the night after your arrival?" Cy reached out and touched her red curls. She leaned into his touch.

"That will be lovely," she said. "Will you be ridiculed for entertaining us at your home instead of spending time at your gentlemen's club?"

Cy's eyes were warm as his lips descended towards hers. "Every gossiping biddy in town will know I prefer your company to that of the drunken, wagering fools at White's."

She smothered her laughter as his lips covered hers. Ivy's hand slid up his broad chest and wrapped around the base of his neck.

He broke the kiss, his face dark with desire. "It is going to be a long two weeks," he rasped.

Chapter IX

Hampshire, England

"I want the chapel on Stanton land filled with lilies and candles. We will require an open carriage to escort the bride and groom to Fenton Hill where the wedding reception will commence," the Duchess commanded imperiously.

The wedding assistant was busily taking notes, scrawling furiously. His cold tea sat untouched on the cart; he would not be able to enjoy it any time soon.

"Ivy, are you disappointed to be getting married here in the country instead of London?" the Duchess asked.

Ivy was staring out the window of the drawing room, unaware of the Duchess's one-sided conversation. She was lost in thought and had a dreamy look on her face.

"*Ivy*," the Duchess barked.

Startled, Ivy finally gave her grandmother her attention, "Yes?"

"Are you satisfied with the arrangements thus far?" The Duchess was determined to enlist her granddaughter's aid in her own wedding.

"Fine," Ivy murmured, looking out the window again.

"Ivy! Will you please pay attention? This is important."

"I am sorry," Ivy answered, but did not sound overly contrite.

The Duchess looked at Charles, the wedding assistant and dismissed him. "Will you excuse us a moment? I must speak with my granddaughter. Please feel free to take refreshment in the kitchen."

Once Charles left, the Duchess looked at Ivy and said, "You seem a bit distracted. Is everything all right?"

"Of course."

"This is your wedding, yet you do not seem not to care one way or the other," her grandmother remarked.

"It is all just a bit overwhelming."

"It is also happening quickly. Usually, an engagement would last at least a year, and that would give us sufficient time to plan. Unfortunately, time is of the essence. Madame LaRue is working day and night to make sure your wedding dress is ready. We can finalize the rest of the preparations from London, but I want to ensure most of the decisions are settled before we leave."

Her gaze softened. Her headstrong granddaughter was falling in love with Stanton, and the Duchess wondered if Ivy realized it. Love was rare in her circle, but it could be found. The Duchess had been in love with her husband; she knew how it could be between a man and a woman, and she wished the same for her granddaughters. She wanted the best for them, despite how their origins had become known to her, and she hoped Ivy and Stanton would find love.

It had been the right decision to introduce them. The debt had been erased, and Ivy would become a countess. Ivy's position would do wonders for Willow's popularity in society.

"Are we finished for the day?" Ivy asked. Her tone was desperate. "I would really like to go see Willow."

The Duchess sighed, realizing if she wanted to accomplish anything at all, she would have to do it without her granddaughter. "You are free to go."

***

Taking a deep breath of reprieve, Ivy left the drawing room and went to the second floor, entering a corner room in the west wing of the manor. Willow stood sketching at an easel as streams of sunlight poured through an open window.

"Have you found your artistic talent yet?" Ivy asked.

Willow turned to her sister and grimaced. "I realize ladies are supposed to be refined and should know how to paint and sketch, but I have yet to master anything of the sort."

Ivy smiled in understanding.

"Sometimes I wish *Maman* had allowed us more time for other endeavors…not just ballet," Willow said.

"You always wanted to master something other than ballet, did you not?"

Willow shrugged. "Unlike you. You always wanted to take the stage."

Ivy smiled sadly. "Now, days are filled with learning how to run a large house and planning menus for balls. Society is going to be exhausting in all the wrong ways."

"You are not excited for London, are you?" Willow asked. During the previous week and a half Ivy had grown solemn and forlorn. "Are you missing Stanton?"

Ivy shrugged, and then sat down in a chair and sighed. "We have only been in England three months. I am already engaged, and about to leave for London to enter society. Do you not feel that our life in Paris is nothing more than a distant memory?"

Willow bit her lip and nodded in agreement.

"I know we had no other options. We had to write Grandmother, but I cannot help feeling that I am caught somewhere in between our old life and this new one."

Willow gripped her sister's hand. "You are not alone, Ivy. I am here. And so is Stanton. Take comfort that you are marrying a kind man."

"You are right."

"Enough wallowing," Willow admonished. "Tell me about your wedding gown."

***

Emily stood in front of a mirror wearing an empire duchess satin wedding gown, encrusted with tiny seed pearls that her Aunt Mildred's modiste had created. Her blonde ringlets were brushed into golden waves, her long neck graceful and fair. Emily's hazel eyes glowed with hatred instead of joy as she stared at herself.

The dress was mocking her, a beautiful reminder that she would not become a countess after all. Enraged, she gripped a delicately embroidered sleeve, and then pulled at it, tearing it into a bundle of thread and fabric. A mass of seed pearls littered the floor. She continued ripping at the dress until it lay in a pile of tattered shreds at her feet.

She breathed in deeply, finally feeling her anger begin to soften, leaving her exhausted. Emily sat down on the edge of her bed in her chemise. She rang the bell for her personal maid, who entered a few moments later and gaped at the mess scattered about the floor. The maid wisely closed her mouth and lowered her eyes as she began to clean up the pile of ruined material.

"What shall I do with this, Miss Emily?" the maid asked when she had gathered every last scrap of fabric, thread and pearls.

"Burn it," Emily said coldly. "And never speak of this incident so long as you live."

***

London, England, June of 1815

Early the next morning, the Duchess and her granddaughters piled into an elegant and sizable carriage. Three coaches followed them, two of which contained all of their clothing and personal items packed into trunks. Their servants shared the third carriage.

Fifteen long hours later, they arrived in front of the Duchess's spacious and luxurious London townhouse, one that had been in the Cavehill family for generations. They had a light dinner and then retired promptly for a much needed night's rest. By the following afternoon, the foyer of the townhouse was flooded with piles of invitations and felicitations.

"What is all this? Is Ivy a smash already!" Willow asked, coming into the drawing room.

The Duchess's brown eyes twinkled with delight. "Absolutely. News travels quickly and everyone is eager to meet the woman who landed the Stanton heir."

Ivy groaned.

"If you think the invitations are overwhelming, wait until you see the wedding gifts that will begin to arrive," the Duchess remarked.

"I do believe my wrist will hurt from all the thank-you notes I will have to write," Ivy drawled.

As the servants unpacked their trunks and set up the household, the ladies called for refreshments. They had not even had their first cup of tea when the butler announced the Earl of Stanton. His tall form graced the doorway.

"Ladies," he said, and then bowed slightly. "Good afternoon. I trust you had a pleasant journey? How are you settling in?"

"Very well, My Lord," Willow said much too reverently, and then began to giggle.

Cy looked at Ivy. "I wonder if I might take my fiancée on an outing to the park?"

The Duchess smiled warmly. Ivy was beginning to see her grandmother smile more frequently, and realized that it changed the entire countenance of the woman's face. She looked twenty years younger. The disharmony and malcontent of Ivy and Willow's arrival had vanished.

"I think that is a marvelous idea. Ivy, do not forget your bonnet and wrap."

Once in the curricle, Cy took the reins, allowing the snowy pair of grays to prance towards the park. Ivy tried to relax, but her thoughts were churning so fast she could barely make sense of them.

The two weeks they had spent apart had given her time to think, and panic had set in days ago. Cy was making a mistake marrying her. She would be an embarrassment to him. Socially beneath him on many levels, she worried that he would be ridiculed because of her background.

"I missed you," he said honestly.

"You did?" she asked, turning a startled gaze to his face.

He looked at her. "Of course. Did you miss me?"

"I…"

"What is going through your mind, Ivy?" he demanded.

She blurted out, "Do you think we are ill-suited?"

Growling like an awakened bear, he grabbed her arms and hauled her towards him, his mouth descending. "How many times do I have to tell you? I chose *you*, Ivy."

"We are in public!" she whispered furiously.

"I do not care. Apparently, I need to prove to you that I want to marry you."

His arms wrapped around her and there was no escape. She sighed, realizing she did not want to. As if he had all the time in the world, Cy placed his lips on hers and explored her mouth with his tongue. She trembled and then kissed him back and enfolded her arms around his neck. He finally broke the kiss, much to her consternation.

"Though I would love nothing more than to continue this, I refuse to ruin your reputation."

Ivy looked around the park. It was still teatime and mostly deserted. She was glad, not yet ready to face a throng of people. She would soon be on display when Cy publicly escorted her to the Greek Ball.

He peered at her, and smiled slowly. "I will kiss you much longer, and much more thoroughly when we are in private. I love that your cheeks are the warm color of a peach and your lips are swollen and rosy."

She sighed in feminine wistfulness as he settled close to her. Taking the reins of his beautiful gray horses, they continued on their drive.

Ivy's fears were laid to rest.

***

Cy was an immaculate host, urbane and sophisticated. He had all the style that had rightfully come with his social position and title. It was a cloak he wore effortlessly across wide, muscular shoulders.

The Count and Countess of Langley were in attendance along with Ivy, Willow and the Duchess. They were seated at the dining room table and Cy watched Ivy's face light with laughter as the Countess whispered something to her. Ivy was at the opposite end of the long table in the hostess's seat, as she would soon be his hostess at every dinner after they were married.

His fiancée was regal and elegant. Her finish was natural; she had always been a diamond. With a little polishing, she now dazzled and shined.

Their wedding was a few months away, and Cy had never been so impatient in his life. He wanted Ivy with him, and he did not want to wait. The time he spent away from her, though it had only been two weeks, had revealed to him how bland and desolate his life had been before her. She was spirited and lovely, and a perfect match for him. He enjoyed reminding her, for she seemed eager to be in his arms. The way she responded to him heated his blood.

"My cousin will be joining us at the Greek Ball," Langley said.

The Countess looked at Willow and remarked, "Beaufort is excellent company. And a wonderful dance partner."

Willow caught the gleam in Countess's eyes and said, "Hopefully I will be able to keep pace with him."

"I think it will be the other way around. Let us hope Beaufort has the constitution to keep up with a Cavehill." The Duchess cackled with laughter.

"Will he be joining us at White's?" Cy asked.

Langley grinned. "I think I can convince him to let you take some of his hard-earned money."

Ivy looked at Cy and asked, "You are a fair gambler, are you not?"

It was a loaded question, and it uncomfortably reminded Cy of his father's gaming debts, many of which had come from White's, an exclusive gentleman's club that existed only for the privileged few.

"Fair," he agreed.

Cy never wanted her to know about his father's debt. He desperately wanted to put it behind him, and after Ivy discovered his brief engagement to Miss Fitzgerald, he did not want her knowing about his agreement with the Duchess. He would not have her think his sole purpose in marrying her had anything to do with money. Even though he would use her dowry to turn his finances around and ensure Ivy's security, he did not want to burden her with his past. Better it stayed there and they looked to the future. He had to admit that he cared for Ivy, and if she learned about his agreement with her grandmother, she might doubt him and his intentions. He wanted them to have a happy, solid marriage.

Most men of his class despised marriage and only went through with it to safeguard the succession of their titles. Very few married for love, or even lasting emotion; that was an elusive quality missing from society relationships almost entirely. Pleasure and companionship were found in the arms of others. Spouses were an unwanted necessity. The Langleys were one of the few happily married couples Cy knew.

Cy had never entertained the idea of having a marriage like theirs, and offering for Miss Emily Fitzgerald had not upset him in the least. Thank God it had not been publicly announced, and he was able to call it off. Miss Fitzgerald was certainly beautiful, but she lacked any true spirit. They would have had a polite life together, and nothing more. Even the idea of dining with the Fitzgerald girl bored him. She had spoken of nothing but the weather and fashion in the few short moments they had spent together. How Cy could have ever thought *that* was all he would require out of a marriage, he would never know. When he met Ivy, he had not realized that she was saving him from a dreary existence. He had begun to hope they might find love.

Cy stared at Ivy again. The candlelight made her hair shimmer, and her eyes seemed dark in the dim light. Her skin was alabaster, and he wanted nothing more than to remove his guests, place Ivy on the dining room table, plow his fingers into her ruby hair and drink from her sweet lips.

Other women pale in comparison, he thought.

Ivy's gaze met his, and when he saw her breath hitch, he did nothing to shield the longing and desire in his eyes. His bold gaze continued to consume her, and he was pleased to note that her hand shook as she raised her glass of wine.

He licked his lips, showing her his want, and he did not care who else knew.

Chapter X

London, England

Three weeks later, it was the night of the Greek Ball. Ivy and Willow peered at the ornate marble columns that graced the edges of the large ballroom, along with colorful silks draped along the windows and hand-carved French doorways. Footmen dressed in Greek dress costumes complete with head laurels circled the room and carried trays of the finest champagne.

"Have you ever seen anything so beautiful?" Willow inquired.

Ivy shook her head and stared at the splendor around her, unaware that she and Willow were the focus of the room's attention. They stood at the top of the plush, red-carpeted stairs waiting to be announced.

Willow was draped in a Grecian silver dress, her blonde curls pinned at her crown. She wore white roses in her hair, and a simple silver ribbon around her neck. Ivy wore a gold gown, and had opted for an out-of-fashion hairstyle. Most of her molten waves had been kept loose, except for the two braids that were pulled back, one of each side of her face.

The butler finally announced their names, and they descended the stairs pretending they were not the cause of commotion. Two young sisters, both exceedingly beautiful and new to the social scene, were more than a little intriguing. When they reached the bottom of the stairs, they were enveloped in a protective group, which consisted of their grandmother, Cy, the Count and Countess of Langley, and Langley's cousin, Lieutenant Roman Beaufort.

Before anyone could get an introduction to the Sinclair sisters, Cy escorted Ivy to the dance floor. The gesture was not lost on the crowd.

Lieutenant Beaufort was tall and handsome, and had an irrepressible grin on his face as he bowed over Willow's hand and asked, "Care to follow suit?"

Willow laughed gaily and let him lead her onto the dance floor.

"You are quite possessive, My Lord," Ivy said breathlessly when Cy twirled her close. "How unusual for a man to be so affectionate in public! Plan on creating a new fashion?"

He grinned lazily back at her. "If you will help."

Ivy's laughter reached many ears.

Cy's black formalwear hugged his wide shoulders. She smiled to herself and thought about all the women in the room who were undoubtedly envious of her.

Once the dance came to an end, Cy led her back to her grandmother. The Duchess was standing with Lord and Lady Dashwell, the hosts of the Greek Ball. Lieutenant Beaufort escorted Willow off the dance floor towards them and bowed, but remained close as he engaged Cy and Lord Dashwell in conversation.

Lady Dashwell turned her attention to Willow and said, "It seems you have captured the interest of the dashing lieutenant. He cannot stop staring at you!"

Willow laughed delightedly. "You are a perfect hostess!"

Lady Dashwell smiled, winked conspiratorially and said, "I must admit, I do like a bit of excitement. If I have anything to say about it, it will be discussed for months to come. Did you know that Lieutenant Beaufort is actually the Marquess of Westonshire's disinherited heir?"

Willow gasped. "Truly?"

Lady Dashwell leaned in close and whispered conspiratorially, "Mr. Beaufort's father married an Irish peasant. The Marquess disinherited his son because of it, and now he completely regrets the decision. Mr. Beaufort's father died, you see, and now the old Marquess needs an heir…"

Willow was fascinated by the story. She gazed at the charming lieutenant, who promptly caught her eye and smiled widely.

Lady Dashwell continued, "He has refused his grandfather, and defied him by becoming an English soldier where he proved himself and was promoted quickly. He fought at Waterloo, under the command of the Duke of Wellington. With the force of one hundred thousand men, they defeated the Emperor, Napoleon."

Willow found herself completely captivated by the lieutenant. Though charming and handsome, there was more to him beneath the surface. Looking at him, she caught him staring at her again. He winked at her, causing her cheeks to flush.

Beaufort strolled towards her, took her hand and led her to the dance floor again.

"Quite presumptuous of you, Lieutenant," she said with a bold smile.

"I took my cue from you, Miss Sinclair," he answered, drawing her close, his hand pressing against the small of her back. "You looked like you wanted to dance with me again."

Willow gasped in mock outrage.

His lazy grin was devastating. "Do not worry. Your secret is safe with me."

***

Ivy was introduced to more people in one night than she could remember meeting in her entire lifetime. Cy was steadily by her side, and took it upon himself to answer pointed questions about their quick engagement and impending marriage with wit that caused most guests to simply cease their implications.

Others noticed Cy's interaction with Ivy, and throughout the evening it was whispered among the guests that every time the Earl of Stanton looked at his fiancée, his eyes softened and a tender look passed over his face.

When Ivy and Cy finally had a moment to take a breath, Cy excused himself to acquire her a beverage. A moment after he left, a tall, impeccably dressed blond man approached her.

He bowed and held her hand a moment longer than was necessary. "Good evening, Miss Sinclair," he crooned arrogantly. "I am Lord Caldwell. Are you enjoying the festivities?"

Momentarily taken aback by the man's abruptness, she finally replied, "I am. Are you enjoying your time here?"

Lord Caldwell smiled and his blue eyes seemed to twinkle. "I would enjoy it so much more if the most beautiful woman at the ball honored me with a dance."

Startled and unsure of how to answer, she tried to think of an excuse and extract her hand. The man was looking at her far too intently, and stood a bit too close for comfort.

"You pay me a great compliment, sir, but I fear I must decline. The Earl of Stanton, my fiancé," she emphasized, "is due back any moment. He will be at a loss if I am gone."

"He is a grown man. He will survive." Lord Caldwell gently, but firmly pulled her towards the dance floor. Not wishing to make a scene, she went with him, and tried to maintain as much distance between them as possible.

Lord Caldwell chuckled upon noticing the distance Ivy was keeping and inflexibly pulled her closer to him. She refused to look up and give him the satisfaction of having cornered her into a dance.

"Do you enjoy riding?" he asked pleasantly.

"I do," Ivy said succinctly.

"Yes, I am sure you do." His voice dropped to a sensual purr. "You were made for riding; lovely and light in the saddle, no doubt. Your carriage erect, your taut thighs controlling your mount."

Her gaze snapped to his, her eyes widening in outrage over his words. He did not seem to be talking about riding a horse at all! "Sir," she hissed. "I would appreciate the chance to sit down. I am a bit tired from all the dancing."

Something moved in Caldwell's blue eyes, and Ivy had a feeling that his social polish was only a thin veneer hiding something dark. However, he played the role of gentleman by inclining his head in assent, and then immediately escorted her off the floor.

Ivy saw Cy waiting for her. He did not look at her; instead his gaze remained trained on Caldwell's face. When Ivy and Caldwell were near, Cy took Ivy's hand in a gesture of protectiveness and pulled her close to his side.

"Thank you for the dance, Miss Sinclair. I would love to see you *ride*," Caldwell said. "Oh, and Stanton, if you ever need someone to keep an eye on your fiancée, you have only to ask." He bowed mockingly.

"My fiancée does not need your company. Now leave. Your presence is ruining Miss Sinclair's evening and mine." His tone was hard and implacable.

Caldwell fumed in silent anger, but wisely made his retreat. Ivy breathed a sigh of relief when she saw Caldwell take his leave of the ball.

"Would you care for a breath of fresh air? Allow me to escort you to the balcony," Cy said, his grip tightening. When they were outside in near solitude, Cy finally demanded coldly, "Why did you dance with Caldwell?"

Ivy gritted her teeth in frustration. She had enough of high-handed men. "He did not give me much choice." She glared up at him. "He dragged me onto the dance floor like you dragged me out here."

Ignoring her pointed statement, he clenched his jaw and said, “Caldwell is *not* a suitable dance partner.”

She crossed her arms over her chest and answered, “I already told you I had no intention of dancing with him, but he was most persistent. I did not care for his solicitous attention. You must believe me.”

“I do,” Cy said, taking a deep breath. “What did he mean by ‘I would love to see you ride’? Does he want to take you riding?”

Ivy’s face flamed. “His tone implied he was referring to something else, I believe.”

Cy’s eyes widened. “That reprobate!”

“Cy, please,” Ivy pleaded. She watched Cy attempt to gain control of his renewed anger.

“Seeing you in his arms made me angry, but hearing what he said to you has made me livid.”

She instinctively took a step away from him and when he noticed, his face softened.

“Come here, Ivy,” he said, gentling his tone. “You do not need to be afraid of me.”

“I know,” she said quietly, taking a tentative step towards him.

Cy pulled her into his arms and his mouth closed over hers. He maneuvered her behind a stone pillar, shielding them from guests. Quickly, he had his hand up her skirt and expertly navigated the many layers of undergarments. He tenderly touched her skin and skimmed his fingers over her slickened bud.

“Cy, no,” she said. “Not here.”

“Yes,” he growled. “I have to touch you.”

He silenced her protest with his mouth, and continued to overwhelm her. Slipping his finger into her moist heat, she convulsed in passion. She whimpered in arousal and denied him nothing.

"Hush, sweet," he said softly as he pulled away from their passionate kiss. "You are safe with me. It has been too long since I have pleasured you, too long since I have seen you writhe in ecstasy in my arms. I cannot have you the way I want you, and so this will have do."

She shuddered, giving in to her desire. It washed over her, nearly knocking her over. She bit his shoulder to keep from crying out. Wrapped in his arms, she sagged against him, letting her breath return to normal. He pulled down her skirts and pressed her head to his chest.

"I think it is time to leave," he said. "I cannot go back to the ball and pretend that I do not want to pleasure you again."

She shivered at his heated words and then nodded in agreement. Leaning her head back, she gazed into his eyes. "I want that, too."

He clenched his jaw, even as he leaned down to give her a quick kiss. "You will surely be the death of me, woman." He sighed. "Let us find your grandmother and sister, and I will escort you to your carriage."

Once Cy made sure they were settled comfortably inside the Duchess's carriage, he said, "I will see you tomorrow. Good night ladies."

As the carriage pulled away, the Duchess looked at Ivy and said, "Where did you disappear to?"

Ivy leaned her head back against the seat. "I was in the powder room," she lied.

"Hmmm. Willow, you seemed to enjoy yourself tonight."

"I did," Willow exclaimed. "Lieutenant Beaufort is a wonderful conversationalist."

Ivy snorted with laughter. "It does not hurt that he is incredibly handsome."

"It is unfortunate that he is untitled," the Duchess remarked.

Willow sighed. "Do you disapprove of him as a prospect?"

"You will have a titled husband, Willow." Her tone brooked no argument. "It is best to forget about Lieutenant Beaufort."

***

Ivy awoke at noon, which was unusual since she was normally an early riser. Stretching lethargically, she then rang for a breakfast tray. She always ate poached eggs and toast in the mornings, as she preferred something more substantial than other young ladies. Half an hour later, as she began to dress, there was a knock on her door. Willow bustled in, full of energy. She plopped down on her sister's bed and smiled.

"Are you still upset over grandmother's announcement that Lieutenant Beaufort is not a worthy escort for you?" Ivy asked without preface.

Willow shook her pretty blonde head. "No. I realize I should not entangle myself so quickly. We only just arrived in London. I need to look over all my prospects. I am sure to find someone Grandmother approves of who is just as a handsome, witty, and sincere as Lieutenant Beaufort."

Ivy raised an eyebrow in disbelief, but said nothing. She had seen her sister interact with the man. There were sparks between them and it had been obvious.

Walking down the stairs and traipsing to the drawing room, Willow and Ivy stopped in the doorway. Dozens of bouquets of flowers graced every available space. The chestnut writing desk had stacks of notes waiting to be read and answered. The sisters looked at each other.

The Duchess entered the room behind the girls and smiled. "These have been arriving all morning."

"For Willow?" Ivy asked.

"Yes, but Stanton sent you a bouquet, Ivy."

"It seems half the *ton* is smitten with Willow," Ivy remarked as she picked up Cy's card, and looked at the ornate bouquet of orchids. She thought about the stolen moments in his arms and blushed.

"This is for Ivy," Willow said as she handed her sister a note and pointed to a bouquet of colorful peonies that had almost been overlooked.

"Who possibly could be sending me an arrangement? I am engaged." Ivy took the note from Willow and opened it. It read: *When will you let me take you riding?*

It was not signed, but she knew whom it was from.

"Ivy? What is it?" Willow asked.

Ivy's eyes were wide as she looked at the Duchess and her sister. "The flowers are from Lord Caldwell."

The Duchess glanced at Lord Caldwell's arrangement of flowers, but did not ask to read the note. "It is a trifle forward knowing you are engaged to the Earl of Stanton. I did see you dancing with Caldwell though. Did you do or say anything to make him think his attentions were welcomed?"

"Of course not!" Ivy spat. "Cy was angry when he saw Lord Caldwell paying me attention. He does not approve of the man."

Willow stared at her sister. "He does not *approve*?"

"Ah. I finally understand," the Duchess said slowly.

"Do explain, please," Willow requested.

"Love, or even lasting affection does not usually occur in upper class marriages. It is not unusual for both men and women to take lovers. Spouses turn a blind eye."

Ivy looked at her grandmother. "Cy is worried I will take a lover?"

The Duchess nodded. "Not just a lover, but a man in his circle to boot, so he is forced to pretend he knows nothing of the liaison. Caldwell's gesture is a discreet way of letting you know that he would be open to sharing his bed with you."

There is nothing discreet about his note!

Distastefully, Ivy picked up the arrangement of peonies and Caldwell's card and promptly rang for Simms. "Take these," she thrust the bouquet into his arms, "and dispose of them. Also, if any other gifts come from Lord Caldwell, please see them taken care of in the same matter."

Simms blinked and then said, "Very good, Miss Ivy. I shall take care of it right away."

"How dare Cy think such a thing!" Ivy nearly yelled as she left the drawing room.

"Should we prepare for an inevitable storm?" the Duchess asked.

"No."

"No?" the Duchess said in surprise.

Willow looked resolute. "We prepare for a tempest."

***

Cy handed his coat and hat to the Duchess of Cavehill's butler, and then said, "Good day, Benson."

"Good day, My Lord," Benson intoned.

"Lovely day, is it not?"

The stoic butler blinked. "Yes, My Lord."

Cy grinned. He was looking forward to seeing Ivy. He was drawn to her like and insect to light and each day it grew harder for him to leave her. These afternoons were not enough. He could not wait for them to be married; he craved more. He wanted to see her first thing in the morning and go to sleep sharing a pillow, the honeyed scent of her in his nose.

"Is Miss Ivy in the drawing room?"

"Yes."

"Good. No need to announce me. I can take care of that myself." He walked down the hallway to the entrance of the drawing room and stopped.

Ivy was pacing back and forth while the Duchess and Willow sat in chairs and watched her with ill-concealed expressions of worry.

"Good afternoon," he called in greeting as he stepped through the doorway.

Tension filled the room as Ivy glanced at him. Her eyes had a dangerous glint and she looked like she was ready to go into battle. Willow appeared nervous, and the Duchess's face quickly smoothed into a polite mask.

"Stanton, good to see you." The Duchess rose from her chair. "Come along, Willow."

"But—" Willow protested.

"*Now.*"

With no choice, Willow followed the Duchess out of the drawing room. Cy frowned in confusion, wondering what he was walking into and why he had been left alone with Ivy.

As soon as the doors closed, Ivy exploded. "Did you want me to stay away from Caldwell because you do not like the man, or because you were afraid he would coerce me into an affair after we were married?"

Reeling in shock, he paused a moment to catch his breath, though Ivy would not let him gain his verbal footing when she queried, "Do you think I will take a lover?"

"Explain what has caused this outburst." His voice was soft, but unyielding.

She looked at him for a long moment. "He sent me flowers. Grandmother explained the meaning behind them."

"Where are they," he growled fiercely.

"I already had them thrown out. I find peonies and the man who sent them revolting." She swallowed. "How could you possibly assume I would ever take a lover? How could you think I wanted him?"

"I never said I did. You jumped to that erroneous conclusion yourself."

She crossed her arms over her chest and looked away from his impassioned gaze. Sighing, he finally took a step closer to her, feeling the anger in the room crackle. She may be irrational at the moment, but she jumbled him up inside so that he could hardly think straight.

"I will share with you some information because I believe you have the right to know. I did wish to shield you from certain unpleasantries, however in the light of our confrontation and Caldwell's intentions, I suppose I should tell you. It is rumored that Caldwell beats women and enjoys it. There is no telling what the man is capable of doing. I am worried about your safety, Ivy. I never thought you would take a lover. Truly."

Ivy blanched. "I had no idea he was actually dangerous. I thought he was simply forward."

Cy took Ivy into his arms and silently crowed in victory when she let him. "I suppose your grandmother has explained society marriages to you?"

"Yes," she admitted. "Will you take a lover?"

"I said I would not."

"No, you said you would not take a mistress. They are different, are they not?"

He growled in exasperation. “I will not take a lover or a mistress. Happy?” She snorted in laughter and his arms tightened around her. “It is your turn to promise me you will not take a lover.”

“I promise,” she said easily.

“When we marry, we pledge fidelity. I take that vow seriously, and you will too.”

“I do not want a life like my mother’s,” she said so softly he almost did not hear her. “She settled for so little. I do not want the same.”

Cy’s heart was beating rapidly from tense emotion, and he wanted nothing more than to comfort and reassure her. Forcing Ivy’s head back, he looked down into her emerald green eyes.

“I will give you all that I am. I will give you my name, my oath to be true to you, and so much more,” Cy said as his lips met hers in an intense, fervent kiss.

“Our fights are quite passionate, are they not?” Ivy asked once they had pulled apart.

Cy’s laugh was strained. There was only so much his body could handle these days. It seemed he only had to look at Ivy to become aroused, something that became increasingly frequent and difficult to stifle.

There was a soft knock at the door, and Willow popped her head in and smiled. Ivy tried to move out of Cy’s arms, but he would not let her. Eventually, she gave up.

“Grandmother wanted to make sure Ivy did not dispose of you prior to the wedding.”

Cy straightened his jacket and smiled. “Not yet.”

Ivy laughed. "If word got around that I dispatched my fiancé, it would be *much* more difficult to acquire a new one."

"Doubtful. There would be a line of wealthy, respectable, titled men outside your grandmother's home in minutes of hearing the news."

Ivy looked at him with humor. "Hmmm. Something to consider."

Chapter XI

London, England

After having left Ivy, Cy walked to White's where he found Caldwell sitting in a corner with a few of his friends. The repugnant man was in the process of enjoying a meal, and Cy grinned menacingly, stalking towards him like a lion ready to pounce on its prey. Caldwell had been too bold with Ivy, and Cy would not stand for it. He approached the group of men quickly and in near silence.

Looking up, Caldwell visibly paled. His two friends had stopped their conversation and watched Cy with fear in their eyes. He paid them little notice.

"Afternoon, Caldwell," Cy gritted, his gaze stony. "Let me get down to the matter at hand. Your attention towards my fiancée is unwelcome."

Caldwell plastered a callous smile on his face as he rose from his chair. Cy hoped Caldwell tried to throw a punch; it would give Cy a good reason to pound him into the ground.

"Worried about some friendly competition?" Caldwell goaded, either not seeing Cy's face had darkened with rage, or too stupid to care.

"If you so much as breathe in Miss Sinclair's direction, I will beat you into a bloody pulp," Cy threatened. He was well within striking distance of Caldwell, but they were at a gentleman's club, and Cy did not want to be the first to fell a blow. However, he was more than prepared to defend himself if Caldwell dared attack.

Caldwell coldly sneered, "Big words. Perhaps she prefers a more refined man, such as myself."

Cy's desire to remain clearheaded evaporated, and his fist connected with the right side of Caldwell's jaw, knuckle to bone. Cy had managed to put some weight behind the punch, and instantly Caldwell's tongue lolled and his eyes rolled in his head. Cy was not a small man, and Caldwell's body went limp and came crashing down onto the chair behind him. His friends reached out to hold him up, but they were too late, and Caldwell's unconscious body fell off the left side of his chair and slumped onto the floor.

Straightening his coat, Cy looked at the other two men, whose mouths were agape in shock, and politely said, "Witherington, Rutherford. Good day."

There was a spring in his step as Cy walked out of White's. He began to whistle.

***

Two weeks later, Cy escorted the Duchess, Willow and Ivy to the opera. They sat in Cy's private box, which had a perfect view of the entire stage. Cy leaned close to Ivy and said, "I have a present for you." He pulled a small, black velvet bag out of his breast pocket and handed it to her.

Gently, she took out a pair of gold-rimmed opera glasses. She looked at him as he said, "They were my mother's. She loved opera and theater. I hope you enjoy them."

Ivy felt her throat tighten and her green eyes misted with emotion. "Thank you. It is a most lovely gift. I will cherish it." She reached over and clasped his hand tightly, wishing they were alone so she could give him a kiss.

"Ivy, is everything all right?" the Duchess asked.

Ivy nodded. "Cy gave me a pair of opera glasses that belonged to his mother. I cannot think of a more perfect present." She said it genuinely, and looked at her fiancé whose face was bathed in a naked look of tenderness.

"May I see them?" Willow inquired. Ivy offered them to her. "They are gorgeous. Well done, sir." She gave the glasses back to Ivy.

The gaslights flickered, signaling guests to their seats, and moments later the curtain rose. They were swept away into a different time and place, but Ivy's mind soon began to wander. She picked up her present, pressed them to her face and let her eyes travel around the opera house. She stilled her movements just as she caught a pair of glasses staring directly at her.

It was Lord Caldwell.

Bile rose in her throat and her head started to throb. He was watching her, motionless.

Cy placed his hand on Ivy's. He must have noticed her hands were ice-cold, because he leaned over and asked, "Are you feeling unwell?"

"No, I am fine. Excuse me one moment, I need to use the powder room," she whispered, leaving the opera box. Quickly, Ivy dashed into the ladies' water closet, sat down on the plush white sofa and tried to compose herself.

Thoughts raced through her mind. Caldwell knew she was engaged. Everyone knew she was engaged; it had been announced in *The Times*. Would Caldwell do more than accost her at balls and stare at her across a room? Was she safe?

When Ivy left the sanctuary of the water closet, she quickly detected the object of her concern leaning casually against a pillar not far from her. She stopped in mid-stride, the breath leaving her body.

"Feeling ill?" he inquired.

"Not at all," she said through a tight throat.

There was a predatory quality about him that was completely disconcerting. His eyes were ice blue, and she felt cold when they were leveled on her.

"I hope you did not leave because of me," he said as he pushed away from the column and striding towards her.

She looked around, glad to see two ushers in red livery standing at the end of the hall. Caldwell would never do anything with witnesses so plainly in sight…would he?

She lied baldly in reply. "Of course not. The music was a trifle loud, and I had a bit of a headache. I just needed a few quiet moments to myself."

There was an amused smile on Caldwell's lips as he came to stand close to her. It was then that she noticed the bruise on his jaw.

"What happened to you?" she demanded.

"Do you care?" he asked huskily.

"Not in the least. I am guessing you had an encounter with my fiancé?" She could not stop her smile.

He sighed. "All because you had to tell him I sent you flowers. Did you enjoy them?"

"As much as one enjoys an incurable malady," she retorted. "I threw them away."

He feigned hurt. "They were *quite* expensive. I hope that is not how you respond to all of my gifts."

Ivy's eyes darted towards him and she said in a mixture of fear and anger, "I do not *want* any gifts from you!"

"When you see their extravagance, you might change your mind, pet."

As he moved to put his hand on her face, the doors swung open. The performance was over and the audience spilled into the common area. She was safe in the presence of so many people, and she sighed in relief when she realized Lord Caldwell had disappeared. She looked for Cy, but he was nowhere to be found. He was probably still in the opera box waiting for her to return, she realized.

When she was able to move through the throng, she took the staircase that would lead back to Cy's opera box. The Langleys had stopped by for a brief conversation before departing. Cy laughed at something Langley said and then finally noticed her presence. Immediately, he left the comfort of his seat and went to her.

"There you are. Have you been in the powder room this whole time?"

Slowly, she shook her head. "Lord Caldwell accosted me outside of it," she said quietly.

Cy's eyes darkened with rage. "Did he touch you?"

"No—almost—but no…he is the reason I went to the powder room. I saw him staring at me from across the way, and his gaze made me…He said he would not stop giving me gifts."

He roughly pulled her to him, and it was enough to turn everyone's focus onto them.

"What happened, Ivy?" Willow asked in a worried tone.

"Caldwell," Cy spat out. "He approached Ivy again. He is becoming rapacious."

"What are you going to do?" the Duchess asked. She looked at Ivy, who was trembling in Cy's arms.

Cy did not answer. Instead, he took hold of Ivy's hand and all but dragged her down the stairs amidst the nobles discussing the opera.

"Do you think he left?" Langley asked, walking in stride next to Cy.

"I hope not," Cy gritted.

"There he is." Langley pointed. Caldwell was conversing with his two friends from White's, Witherington and Rutherford.

"Caldwell!" Cy lashed out. The man stopped in mid-conversation and stared at Cy with glacial blue eyes. "I demand satisfaction at tomorrow's dawn."

Witherington sputtered, "Come now, Stanton. What is all this talk of satisfaction?" His jowls flapped ridiculously as he spoke, his face beading with sweat.

Caldwell looked bored, and foolishly so. "I have not the faintest idea why you are demanding such a thing, Stanton. This has all been a misunderstanding."

The lobby of the opera house had grown quiet as patrons watched Cy's tête-à-tête with Lord Caldwell.

"Surely your fiancée told you she enjoys my attentions. Otherwise, what reason would I have to pursue her?" Caldwell taunted. He then looked past Cy and smiled at Ivy who gasped.

Ivy's hand was still clasped in Cy's, and his grip tightened as his voice shook with anger, "I will see you at dawn in Hyde Park, Caldwell. Twenty paces with a pistol. If you do not show, I will assume you are a sniveling coward. I already know you have no honor, but I doubt you would want to be considered a weakling as well." Cy ground his last words out through a clenched jaw.

"I am no coward, Stanton. I name Rutherford as my second."

Rutherford, a tall, gangly man fingered his collar nervously and began to look ill. He swallowed audibly.

"Langley will act as mine." Cy turned abruptly, taking Ivy with him. He had not let go of her hand for even a moment.

The surrounding crowd blazed with gossip, speculating on the outcome of the duel. It was not until Cy and his party was outside that Ivy spoke. "What are you doing?"

"It is about honor, Ivy, and Caldwell has none. He must be stopped before he hurts you. Am I to wait until it is too late?"

Ivy bit her lip as she buried her face in his chest and whispered, "I do not want you to get hurt."

"Take comfort, Miss Sinclair," Langley said. "Stanton is an excellent shot."

It only made Ivy more concerned.

"I will come to your house after the duel is over," Cy said to the Duchess.

She nodded. "Well done, Stanton. Caldwell is out of control."

Cy escorted them to the Duchess's waiting carriage. "I will see you soon," he promised Ivy as he closed the door.

When the coach took off, the Duchess said with a little too much force, "All will be well."

Willow agreed. "Of course. That man can handle anything. I would not want to be Caldwell." She laughed, but it was strained.

"Why must he do this?" Ivy asked. "It is dangerous."

"You heard what he said about honor, Ivy. Stanton is a gentleman. He is protecting what is his," the Duchess explained.

Ivy wondered what the dawn would bring.

***

As streaks of dawn appeared, Cy stood in a loose white shirt, fawn colored breeches and brown riding boots. He glared at his opponent, who was trying to ignore Cy as he made himself ready. Witherington and Rutherford stood next to Caldwell and spoke in low voices, no doubt trying to puff up Caldwell's nerve.

Langley looked at Cy. "Are you sure you want to do this?"

Cy nodded curtly. "The man must be stopped. He has made advances towards my fiancée, and he is dangerous."

Langley wisely did not say a word. Even Cy knew he was unreachable in his anger, his vision blurry red, and there was be no reasoning with him. Cy had never gone to such lengths to protect a woman. He cared about Ivy, more than he had ever cared for anyone.

"Is the doctor here?" Cy asked.

"Yes, and he has assured us of his tact, as you requested."

Cy smiled without humor and said sarcastically, "Because *that* is our biggest concern. I cannot trust Caldwell to act with decorum."

When both parties were ready with their pistols in hand, they approached each other slowly and stood back to back. Witherington and Langley were off to the side fifteen feet away and watched, ready to intercede if necessary.

"You are men of honor," Langley called out. "You will do well to remember it."

Cy nodded and clenched his jaw. He was not worried about *his* honor; it was Caldwell's he was concerned about.

"*Count it!*" Caldwell spat, apparently ready to settle the matter.

Light finally peeked through the trees as the two men stood back to back. Caldwell and Cy had agreed that Langley would count twenty paces, and then each man would turn and shoot. There was a good chance that one or both of them would be killed or seriously injured.

Langley started the count.

"One!"

Langley's voice rang out in the clear, early morning.

"Two!"

A cool breeze stirred the leaves that crunched beneath Cy's feet.

"Three…Four…Five!"

Cy was tense, ready, and worried about Caldwell. How would a repugnant creature react in an honorable challenge?

"Six…Seven!"

Just as they got to the nineteenth pace, Caldwell began to twist.

"Stanton!" Langley called out in warning as Caldwell moved prematurely. Cy spun around as fast as he could, but he was not quick enough. Caldwell had a head start; he pointed his pistol and fired.

A white-hot bullet tore through Cy's side, under his ribs, and settled just below the skin on his back. With his free hand, he grasped his side and tried to shoot with the other, but burning pain coursed through his veins like an injection of poison, and he fired hastily. He had no way of knowing if he hit his target, and before the smoke even cleared, he was overtaken by darkness.

***

Numerous pairs of hands held him down as the dull ache below his ribs turned into searing pain. Gauze was shoved into his wound, and he remembered he had been shot. He screamed in agony when he felt cold metal pierce his skin, and began to buck like a wild stallion. He managed to open his eyes off and on, only to see cloudy visions of Langley, and the doctor from the duel, head bent, digging into his side.

Blessedly, he passed out again.

Chapter XII

London, England

After the opera, Ivy refused to go to sleep; the Duchess and Willow kept her company in the salon. Though it would not be for many hours, they waited for news of the duel to reach them. As night wore on, Ivy's apprehension grew. When dawn finally arrived, the Duchess convinced her to eat something, but Ivy's stomach was a bundle of nerves. Until she knew Cy was safe, she would not be calm.

A little after the clock chimed eight, there was a pounding on the Cavehill door. Ivy did not wait for Benson to answer it.

"Get your cloak," the Count of Langley said to Ivy urgently, coming into the foyer.

Willow and the Duchess had entered the hallway. Doing as bid, Ivy wrapped her cloak around her. She was still in her formal gown from the night before. She had not wanted to waste time changing in case she had to leave suddenly.

"What happened?" Ivy demanded.

Langley's jaw clenched. "He has been shot."

Willow gasped, and the Duchess pressed a hand to her heart.

Ivy's face paled. "How bad is it?"

Langley's eyes were filled with sorrow. "It does not look good. We must go."

They rushed from the house and left Willow and the Duchess alone, shocked and motionless.

Once Ivy and Langley were seated in his carriage and on their way dodging through the early morning traffic, Ivy asked, "What happened to him, My Lord?"

Langley shook his head and gritted out, "Caldwell got to pace nineteen and turned early. He nearly shot Stanton in the back, but I called out a warning and Stanton managed to turn. He was not quick enough, and the bullet went into his side."

Ivy felt rage boiling inside her unlike any she had ever experienced. "Where is the *fils de pute*?"

"The commotion gave Caldwell enough time to run away. I wanted to pursue him, but Stanton was bleeding badly and needed help. Stanton is at my townhouse. The doctor dug out the bullet and stitched his side, but now he is feverish and the doctor is worried about infection."

The carriage stopped and Langley jumped out before the footman had even opened the door. He helped Ivy down and then escorted her inside. Ivy followed him up the stairs and into a lavish guest room. The Countess sat by the bed, her face distressed.

Cy was lying in an opulent bed, but the sheets were covered in blood, and patches of soiled linen were strewn across the floor. Ivy immediately rushed to him. She felt his flushed cheek, and observed him as he began to mutter in delirium.

"The doctor left a short while ago and asked that we watch him closely," the Countess whispered.

Ivy's heart ached as she said, "Thank you for taking care of him. I will stay by his side now."

She immediately went to a chair next to the bed and removed her cloak, ready to stay until Cy awoke. She leaned over him, wanting to ensure that he was breathing. When she was satisfied, she sat down and then looked inquisitively at the Count and Countess of Langley. They stared back at her, their faces dazed.

"I will call for clean sheets at once," Langley said finally. "Ring if there is any change."

Ivy nodded, but did not say anything; she was too focused on Cy. His skin was hot to the touch, and his forehead felt like it was on fire.

She closed her eyes and finally gave in to her worry as a tear rolled down her cheek. *He must be safe*, she thought fearfully. She did not know what she would do without him. She cared for him, more than she had wanted to admit. Cy was more than a charming man of the *ton* that she was fortunate enough to marry. He was unique and caring, and he allowed her to see who he was below the surface. There was no deception, no guile in him. There was trust and honesty between them.

And now, just as they had begun their life together, he was in danger of being snatched from her like a kite from a child's hands.

Cy, you wonderful idiot, she thought.

He was such a principled man that he had decided to protect her honor and entered into a duel against a gutless scoundrel. He had been shot, and now he was desperately clinging to life in a blood-soiled bed.

She knew at that moment she was in love with him.

***

He smelled her long before he could open his eyes. She smelled like rain and dark honey.

"Ivy," he whispered, his fevered mind searching for her face behind burning eyes. He had never been so hot in his life. His body was blazing from within, as though he was trapped in a tomb of unbearable heat.

Something cool pressed against his brow, and he turned towards it.

"Get me Ivy," he gritted out. Flames licked along his side.

"I am here. You will not die," a melodic voice whispered.

A small, feminine hand touched his forehead, and he breathed a sigh of relief. In his delirium, he was able to conjure a vision of her. Brilliant red hair falling across her naked, magnolia skin, and her green eyes gleaming like wet leaves in springtime. Her smiling rosy mouth coming towards him and settling on his lips, giving him succor, dousing the flames within.

***

Just as the sun had begun to set, Ivy was jarred awake. Her neck hurt from falling asleep in the chair again, but she was instantly alert.

"Ivy," Cy whispered softly. She rushed to his side, surprised to find him awake. His gray eyes were lit with pain, but he managed to smile. "You came."

Gently, she sat down on the bed next to him and searched for his hand among the many covers. When she found it, she squeezed it lightly. "Of course I came, you dolt," she said affectionately. Her eyes began to prick with tears, and she was unable to stop them from falling down her cheeks.

Cy reached out to caress her face, but his hand fell. "I want to touch you, but I do not have the strength, and my side is throbbing."

Ivy stopped crying and moved so she could pull back the covers.

"What are you doing?" Cy asked in shock.

"I want to see the wound."

"This is improper." Cy tried to fend her off, but his meager strength was waning.

"Improper? You think *this* is improper? Shall we go down the list of what has occurred between us? Let me see it," she demanded again.

He gave in, and she pulled up his nightshirt and tried to disregard a muscular leg as she sought to uncover the dressing. The skin around the stitches was angry and red.

"I am sending for the doctor," Ivy said as she picked up the bell to ring for a maid.

"I do not need the doctor," Cy said tiredly.

She glared at him. "It is my turn to be the overprotective, tyrannical fiancée." The maid arrived and Ivy said, "Tell the Count of Langley that Cy is awake and to send for the doctor. Also, send up some broth and fresh water."

When the maid left to do Ivy's bidding, Cy said with an exhausted smile, "You give orders like a general at war. You will make a fine countess."

She smiled. "*Your* countess." Her lips began to quiver with emotion again. Her own weariness and tension were overpowering her. "You were almost killed, Cy."

"Come here," he said gently.

Ivy eagerly went to him, and when he wrapped an arm around her she sobbed, releasing every ounce of worry and fear that had built up in the days since he had been shot. He pressed his lips to her forehead. She pulled back just as the Count and Countess of Langley entered the room.

Ivy tried to move away from Cy, but he kept his arm firmly around her. Langley raised an eyebrow and said, "You gave us quite a scare. Good to see you awake, Stanton."

"I had incentive to wake up," Cy replied as he nodded towards Ivy who was blushing.

The Countess smiled tenderly at Cy and Ivy and said, "We sent for the doctor and he should be here soon. I also sent the Duchess a note apprising her of his condition and requested that you stay with us while Stanton recovers. I doubt you will leave his side."

"I cannot let him out of my sight, for trouble seems to find him," Ivy quipped.

"Valid point, my dear," Cy said.

The doctor arrived, changed his dressings and pronounced Cy was on his way to making a full recovery. He suggested bed rest for at least a week and plenty of broth and tea, but overall the prognosis was good.

When they were finally alone, Ivy picked up the bowl of broth and spoon the maid had brought up and said, "You are going to eat every bit of this."

"You are not going to feed me," Cy protested.

She grinned cheekily. "If you can take the spoon from me, I will let you feed yourself."

When he made a move, he grimaced and collapsed against the pillows. He was panting, out of breath.

"That is what I thought. No one has to know that I fed you like a baby."

He growled in frustration, but let her spoon-feed him. When he was finished eating, she took the bowl, placed it on the tray and kissed his forehead, which was still a bit warm.

He was asleep before she made it to the door.

After Ivy ate her own dinner on a tray in the guest room, she took a luxurious bath. She had not left Cy's side in days, and she needed to rest.

A short while later, Ivy slid into bed, her head hit the pillow, and she slipped into her own blissful sleep.

***

"Where is Caldwell?" Cy demanded.

He was sitting in Langley's library, enjoying time out of bed. He hated feeling like an invalid, and though Ivy had barely left his side and had entertained him with cards and reading, he was ready to regain his independence and mobility.

Langley shook his head. "I have hired investigators to track him down. I also went to see

Rutherford and Witherington, and both of them swear he has not been in contact with them. They are quite appalled by their friend's lack of honor."

"He will need money at some point," Cy said heatedly. "And when he does, we will have our trail."

"I know you are angry, but do not go looking for him. He almost killed you once. Let him come back. He will eventually, and when he does, we will be ready for him."

Cy's eyes turned steely gray, but he nodded curtly.

There was a knock on the door and Langley called out, "Come in."

Ivy popped her head in and smiled. "Are you two finished with your business? I want to walk with Cy around the garden."

Langley leaned back in his chair and smiled. "Do not let me detain you, then."

Once Ivy and Cy were out in the sunshine, Cy immediately brought Ivy into his arms and kissed her passionately.

"I have been wanting to do that for days," Cy said as he pulled away from her. He loved the way her cheeks flushed after they kissed.

"Finally had the energy to dedicate to it?" she quipped and then sobered. "I never did thank you for avenging my honor."

"I never thanked you for staying by my side while I recovered," he answered, his hands rising to hold her face.

She licked her lips delicately, as if she wanted nothing more than to have his mouth on hers again.

He obliged and buried his lips in hers, wanting to make up for lost time.

"Do not ever terrify me like that again," she said, tearing her mouth from his. She wrapped her arms around him and hugged him tightly. He winced at the pain, but remained silent for Ivy's sake.

"Oh, sorry. I forgot about your injury." She pulled back when she realized she had pressed his still tender wound.

His grimace turned to a genuine smile. "I am sorry to have worried you, but you are going to be my wife. I could not let Caldwell get away with his pursuit of you," he said possessively.

"You were hurt because of me."

He heard the guilt in her voice and wanted to ease it. "Ivy, I would never forgive myself for not protecting you."

"And I could never live with myself if I was the cause of your death!" Ivy shouted.

He kissed her again, wanting to distract them both from their fears. Cy's heart was beating rapidly when he finally lifted his head and gazed into emerald green eyes that were shimmering with suppressed tears. He realized he was dangerously close to being in love with this wild, spirited woman who wanted to take care of him just like he took care of her. His heart eased, and he nearly sighed with contentment.

Chapter XIII

London, England, late June of 1815

"You should go to the Marchioness of Clinton's garden party," Cy said to Ivy the next day.

"I am not sure. How are you feeling?"

He nearly growled in frustration. "Stop playing nurse, I am fine. You need to go out and enjoy the afternoon."

"On one condition," she said. "Promise me you will not attempt any strenuous physical activities."

He raised an eyebrow and grinned roguishly. "What sort of activities are you referring to?"

She blushed. "Promise me," she demanded.

He laughed and said, "I promise. I will spend the afternoon reading in Langley's library. Is that mellow enough for you?"

With one last look in his direction, Ivy left him and met the Countess in the foyer. She would meet her grandmother and sister at the garden party and then return home with them. There was no longer any reason to stay at the Count and Countess of Langley's townhouse; Cy was healed.

When Ivy and the Countess arrived at the Marchioness's townhouse, they were shown to the solarium. It was large and spacious with tall plants and ferns gracing every available space. The windows were open, letting in the afternoon breeze and watery sunlight. It had rained the night before and the smell of fresh air mingled with the scent of plant life.

Greeting their hostess, they made the rounds. When Ivy saw her sister and grandmother, she immediately went to them. The past week, they had visited the Langley townhouse while Cy was recuperating, but Ivy had spent little time with them. Loath as she was to admit it, Cy had been correct. It had done her good to get out and socialize.

"I had no idea the point of a garden party was to judge other people's fashion," Willow said in amazement as she took a drink of lemonade. "I passed three woman that were ripping to shreds another woman's choice of dress."

The Countess laughed. "That is the point of a lot of social gatherings, my dear."

"Lady Gertrude should never have worn the pink gown. And Miss Victoria's hair looks like it was pinned by the stableman," Willow said in a mocking voice.

Ivy laughed. "You are such a comic, Willow."

Willow inclined her head. "Why thank you, dear sister."

"I wary of being able to teach you both any manners," the Duchess remarked dryly but then spoiled her admonishment with a smile. She excused herself to speak to her friend, Lady Stanhope.

News of the duel between the Earl of Stanton and Lord Caldwell was still a juicy topic of discussion. No one asked Ivy about it directly because it was not considered polite, but curious glances were thrown at her all afternoon. It took every ounce of willpower for people to stem their interest.

"Ignore them," the Countess whispered. "They will forget about it soon."

"Let us hope," Ivy mumbled.

"We should start a rumor so everyone has something else to talk about!" Willow suggested.

"Such as?" the Countess queried.

"How should I know?"

"You really have not thought this plan through, have you?" Ivy said with a smile.

Willow grinned. "Not even a little bit."

***

The Sinclair sisters chatted vivaciously with the Countess of Langley, as Emily's hazel eyes narrowed on the stunning and elegant redhead. The young woman with entrancing green eyes laughed, and it made Emily dig her nails into her palm.

Emily hated her.

The garden party guests were abuzz, conversing about the duel that the Earl of Stanton had fought against Lord Caldwell. No one was completely clear on the facts, and Emily was dying to find out the entire story. Perhaps she would enlist the aid of Mathilda and Alyssa to find out the truth.

Wanting to officially meet the woman who had managed to lure the Earl away from her, Emily approached the group of women and pasted a smile on her face, glad she had dimples that made her appear sweet and nonthreatening. She had worn a lilac gown that showed off her coloring and emphasized her youthful, curvy physique.

"Good afternoon, My Lady," Emily said pleasantly to the Countess, giving an effortless curtsy. She turned her attention to the redhead, abhorring the woman's brazen hair that made her glow like a candle in darkness. Though Emily knew herself to be lovely, she could not compete with the outright beauty of Miss Sinclair.

"Good afternoon, Miss Fitzgerald. I thought you were in Paris," the Countess said.

"I only just returned," Emily explained and then turned her attention to the two women who she had yet to meet.

"Miss Emily Fitzgerald, may I present Miss Ivy Sinclair and her sister, Miss Willow Sinclair."

Emily flashed what she knew was a dazzling smile and looked at the Earl's fiancée. "How lovely to meet you both. I have been dying to make your acquaintance since you arrived. Are you enjoying your time in London?"

The redhead opened her mouth to reply, but her sister interjected and answered for her, "London is wonderful. We have recently been to the opera, and it was a most enjoyable experience."

"I do love the opera. And London." Emily's voice cooled considerably when she said, "One can find many *passing* diversions in the city."

It was a subtle cut, but a cut nonetheless. Emily wanted to draw blood, and eviscerate the woman that society claimed the Earl loved. There were rumors of how he looked upon his fiancée; and it made Emily tremble with fury.

The Countess smiled sweetly and said, "Miss Fitzgerald, have you read about Miss Sinclair's engagement to the Earl of Stanton?"

"I think I skimmed it…Engagements can be broken, you know. Congratulations. I do hope you both find some measure of happiness." She turned and swept away.

The rest of the afternoon, Emily fumed. She was unable to keep her attention off of Miss Ivy Sinclair. The woman was only welcomed into polite society because her grandmother was the Duchess of Cavehill. Ivy Sinclair was nothing more than the illegitimate daughter of a duke! How had she managed to snatch the Earl away from Emily, the daughter of a wealthy baron? Anger twisted in Emily's stomach. She loathed the woman for taking the Earl from her, but she hated the Earl for his rejection and choosing a woman so clearly beneath him.

Emily was an only child, and her parents doted on her. With the exception of the Earl, she had gotten everything she had ever wanted. With Miss Sinclair's appearance, Emily had lost a fiancé and the potential title of a countess. It was an insult she would not forget.

"Miss Fitzgerald! How lovely to see you!" Lady Baker said in greeting.

"It is lovely to see you as well," Emily replied politely.

"We missed you at the Greek Ball, but I do know how much you love Paris. Is that a new gown?" Lady Baker spouted a series of mixed statements and questions as she linked her arm through Emily's and began walking with her.

"It is," Emily said, feeling temporarily soothed and somewhat distracted. "Brand new from my recent trip."

"You must show the Countess of Hartford and Lady Essex. They will want one just like it."

Emily smiled, and feelings of happiness were restored as the compliments continued, but then she caught a glimpse of Miss Sinclair engaged in conversation with the Duchess of Cavehill and Lady Stanhope.

Stewing in resentment, Emily glared at the woman, wishing for revenge.

***

Late that night, back in the Duchess's townhouse, Willow sat on Ivy's bed talking about their afternoon. They were eating apple tarts snuck from the kitchen and drinking hot chocolate. The moon glowed through the window, and Ivy lit candles so they could move around without bumping into things.

"Can you believe Miss Fitzgerald?" Willow asked as she took a sip of her chocolate.

Ivy shook her head. "Only women of quality can give an insult without it sounding like an insult. They prefer to deliver snide comments, each like a small lash against you. One or two does not hurt, but after many, you feel the pain." They were silent for a moment and then Ivy said, "She is pretty."

"She is, yes," Willow agreed tentatively.

"It is hard to believe Cy was ever engaged to such a woman."

"The engagement was barely an engagement," Willow reminded her. "Besides, I think the Earl is quite fond of you."

"Hmmm," Ivy said. "I am quite fond of him."

"Only fond?" Willow pressed.

"More than fond," Ivy allowed. "He is wonderful. Protective, charming, sincere, witty, urbane. He is everything a woman could hope for in a future husband."

"You are looking forward to the wedding," Willow stated with a smile.

"Yes, I am."

"Has he kissed you?"

Ivy's face heated as she nodded.

"You love him, do you not?"

"I do," Ivy admitted.

"Mother would like him."

"Very much." She paused in thought. "Do you ever think Mother resented the fact that the Duke could not marry her?"

"She never said anything about it if she did," Willow responded, reaching for Ivy's uneaten tart. "She seemed content with life. She enjoyed ballet and she loved us." Willow stared hard at her sister, whose face was a canvas of conflicting emotions. "She knew you did not mean it, Ivy."

Ivy's green eyes were troubled. "At the time, I meant every word I said. I thought she was nothing more than a beggar awaiting scraps. I suppose one cannot look back and wish for things to be different. Look where we are now."

"It is hard to believe, is it not? I do not know what we would do if we were still in Paris."

Ivy sighed. "I never would have met Cy and fallen in love."

Willow looked at her sister. "Have you told him?"

Ivy chuckled. "I thought I would let him fully recover from the duel before I clobber him with my declaration of feelings."

Willow laughed. "Timing really is everything, is it not?"

***

An ornate, antique vase hit the wall with a resounding crash, shattering in a thousand pieces like a dream lost when one is startled out of a sound sleep. The young woman who threw it breathed heavily, her face flushed and her hazel eyes alight with anger.

"Bitch!" she spat furiously.

Footmen and maids who heard the commotion did not even raise an eyebrow at the foul language or tantrum being thrown by their young mistress. They were accustomed to her fits of rage and were compensated enormously by the girl's parents as a means to ensure that word did not spread about her behavior. Society was under the distinct impression that she was a polite, well-bred girl, almost to the point of being bland and uninteresting. Underneath the façade, however, was a spoiled rich child with a high level of self-entitlement and lack of self-control.

The door to the salon opened and a stout, matronly woman entered the room.

"What is it, my love?" Emily's mother, Lady Fitzgerald stood in the doorway, immune to another daily episode.

"*This!*" Her daughter held up an invitation. "The Countess of Langley is throwing a ball in honor of the engagement between the Earl of Stanton and Miss Ivy Sinclair."

"The Countess of Langley throws lovely balls," Lady Fitzgerald said innocently.

Emily's color deepened as her fury raged. "I know. It should have been *me*!"

Her mother blinked owlishly. "What should have been you, dear?"

Emily gritted out, "The ball should have been in *my* honor! The Earl of Stanton should have a fought a duel on my behalf!" Emily had finally learned the story in its entirety through Mathilda, who had heard it from an impeccable source.

Lady Fitzgerald did not reply to the statement, choosing instead to ask, "Am I to assume you will not be attending?"

Emily glared at her mother. "Of course I am going." She smiled malevolently. "And I intend to make it the most interesting event of the Season."

***

Ivy was reading in the corner of the Cavehill library, enjoying her solitude while Willow and their grandmother were out shopping. It seemed like such a long time since Ivy had any spare time to read for pleasure and relax in the confines of a comfortable room. At the moment, there were no demands on her time, and she was enjoying every minute of her freedom.

The Count and Countess of Langley's Ball to celebrate Ivy's engagement to Cy was that evening, and Ivy was looking forward to dancing the night away with her fiancé. His wound was healed, and she wanted him to hold her tight, whirl her around the room, and kiss her until she was senseless. Her blood heated at her dangerous thoughts.

"Miss Ivy," Benson said. He unintentionally startled her from thoughts of Cy, but then announced, "The Earl of Stanton is here."

Stomach fluttering, Ivy closed her book, not at all surprised Cy was paying her a visit. It had become customary for him to call in the early afternoon, and then come again at night to escort her and her family out for the evening's festivities.

"Hello," she said with a smile as Cy walked into the library.

"Good afternoon. Your yellow gown is as sunny as your disposition."

"Thank you," she replied breathlessly due to Cy's appreciative gaze. "I am happy to see you."

He looked pleased by her pronouncement. "You are?"

Her cheeks flushed and she nodded. "I also think you look quite handsome in your brown jacket."

"Stop," he said with a teasing smile. "Your compliments are going to my head."

"What if I admit that I want you to take me into your arms and greet me with a kiss?"

He shook his head even as he stalked towards her. "You are sinful." He leaned down and gently brushed his lips against hers. When he pulled back, she was frowning.

"Much too short, My Lord."

Laughing, he said, "You are distracting me from my real purpose in coming here. I have a present for you."

Ivy protested lamely, "You have given me so many gifts already."

"This should have been given to you the moment we became engaged."

He pulled out a small, black leather jewelry box and handed it to her. She opened it, revealing a beautiful solitaire diamond with small diamonds encircling a gold band.

"I had it commissioned in France. That is why it took so long to get here," Cy explained when Ivy failed to react.

Slowly, she raised her eyes to his. They were shining with tears. "It is so beautiful," she whispered.

He took the ring and gently slid it on her finger. She leaned over and kissed him on the lips.

When they parted, he grinned and said, "If you cry at receiving your betrothal ring, I shudder to think how you will react when I give you the jewels that belonged to my great-grandmother."

She smiled with tears still in her eyes and asked playfully, "Are they worth crying over?"

"Bawl worthy," he corrected.

She laughed, wiped a tear from her face with her hand and then stared at the ring again. "It really is quite stunning."

"Not as stunning as you," he responded, as he peered into her eyes.

Her cheeks flamed under his intense gaze. Their tender moment dissolved as they heard voices in the hallway. Ivy watched footmen carrying dress boxes past the open door and up the stairs.

"Good afternoon, ladies," Cy said to the Duchess and Willow who came into the library. "Productive outing?"

Willow grinned. "Very."

"Glad to hear it. Now, if you will excuse me, I have some things to see to before the ball tonight. I will come at seven to escort you to the Langleys'."

When he left, the Duchess asked, "Did you two have a nice visit?"

Ivy nodded and held out her hand to display her ring. "He came to give me this."

Willow gasped in awe, and the Duchess peered at Ivy's engagement ring and nodded as she said, "Exquisite."

"It will go perfectly with the dress you are going to wear to the Langleys' Ball," Willow said.

"I imagine it will go well with every dress you own," the Duchess remarked with a laugh.

Ivy's grin stretched from ear to ear. It was going to be a wonderful night.

***

Cy walked into White's, planning to meet the Count of Langley and his cousin, Lieutenant Beaufort, for a few hours before the ball. He saw two other likable men in his circle and said, "Good afternoon, Hargrove, Essex. Would you care to join Langley, Beaufort and me for a few rounds of cards?"

Essex fingered his cravat and said, "So sorry old boy, but I am afraid we were about to leave." They got up quickly and scampered out the door.

Cy's brow furrowed in confusion. News of the duel had finally died down, and Cy wondered what could have caused the two men to run away from him like he had an incurable, catching disease.

He found Langley and Beaufort in the corner enjoying a quiet afternoon brandy. "I just tried to invite Essex and Hargrove over for a few hands of cards, and they could not leave my company fast enough."

Langley and Beaufort exchanged a look.

"Is there something I should know?"

Langley sighed and said, "May I speak frankly in front of Beaufort?"

"Of course."

"Word got out about your father's debt."

Cy cursed.

Beaufort cleared his throat. "It seems people think you are living entirely on credit, and that you do not have any means to pay off his debt."

"That was never true. I could have liquidated everything I own to pay the debt, but then been left with nothing," Cy explained. "When I became engaged to Ivy, the debt was forgiven."

Beaufort leaned back in his chair and thought a moment. "And now there is no refuting the rumor without telling the world the intimate details of your situation?"

Cy grimaced. "Not without Ivy finding out that I originally planned to marry her to rid myself of a long-standing family debt. It would destroy our relationship, not to mention Ivy's fledgling relationship with her grandmother."

"Who could have known about the debt aside from the Duchess of Cavehill and Langley? Did Fitzgerald know?" Beaufort asked.

Cy nodded. "We had discussed the situation in great detail. He knew I was no spendthrift. I was going to use his daughter's dowry to pay the debt. My business investments are turning a profit. It would only be a matter of time before my former wealth was restored."

"Do you think it was Fitzgerald himself that told?" Langley queried.

Cy shook his head. "Fitzgerald assured me of his discretion, and when I told him about the Duchess's offer, he agreed it would be best to dissolve the engagement with his daughter."

"Do you think he explained to Miss Fitzgerald why the engagement was called off?" Beaufort inquired.

"I do not think so, since it was none of her concern. Honestly, I did not think she cared one way or the other. She never showed me any partiality."

"Maybe the chit really wanted to marry you," Langley offered.

"Perhaps, but I still do not think Fitzgerald would be so careless as to entrust information about my personal finances with his young, title-chasing daughter," Cy said. "And you are correct. I never felt that she cared one way or another about me, but it is possible I was mistaken. It is also possible she was upset about not becoming a countess."

"Absolutely," Beaufort remarked cynically.

Cy knew Beaufort had become a bit jaded due to women fawning over him for his potential title. His grandfather was still trying to make him his legal heir, but Beaufort refused to live a life of hypocrisy. He did not want to marry a woman who wanted nothing more than the prestige of what his title would bring her.

"I still think it started with Fitzgerald. If not him, then possibly his daughter," Langley said.

Cy thought for a moment. "I suppose it is possible, but I really doubt it."

"We must find out," Beaufort said.

"Yes," Cy agreed. "Ivy cannot know about this."

"You love her, do you not?" Langley asked.

"Yes, I love her," he replied simply.

Beaufort quirked an eyebrow. "Did you tell her?"

Cy threw his friend a look and replied, "One problem at a time, my friends."

Chapter XIV

London, England, July of 1815

Cy's eyes scanned the ballroom, his mind barely registering the splendor of the decorations. Long tables set with food and drink and the whirling couples dancing to a waltz did not distract him from his cause. He was looking for the Duchess in hopes that he might have a few minutes alone to inform her of the situation that had arisen.

Earlier in the afternoon, he had sent a note to the Duchess's townhouse stating an urgent matter had occurred, and he would be unable to escort them to the ball, but would meet them there.

The gentlemen had come up with a plan. Beaufort was to get close to Miss Fitzgerald, gain her trust and query her for information to find out all that she knew. They were certain she was the culprit, but they did not know how she came about the information.

Langley wanted to tell his wife about the plan thinking they could enlist her help to ensure Ivy did not hear the gossip. Cy was adamant that the less people who knew the entirety of the situation the better.

Cy was not concerned that news of his father's debt had spread like wildfire. He was, however, worried that Ivy would hear the rumors and wonder about his true motives in marrying her. She was a smart woman, and she would put the pieces together. Realizing it was a lot of trouble to go through to keep her in the dark, he knew the *ton* and how they would react. Ivy would be humiliated and ridiculed, and Cy would not let that happen. Ivy trusted him to take care of her, and he would.

Ivy entered with her grandmother and Willow, and even from a distance her eyes seemed to glow, and they matched the emerald green ball gown she wore. Her molten curls were pinned up, her graceful neck displayed for the entire world to see. It was an instant reminder of what Cy stood to lose, and it propelled him to action. He immediately went to her side, grasped her hand and boldly kissed it. When she smiled, anger twisted in his gut. He loved her, but if she found out the truth, she would doubt his feelings.

"I am sorry I could not escort you this evening. Something came up at the gentlemen's club." Though it was true, he hated to lie by omission.

She waved away his excuse. "Do not concern yourself. We are together now."

Lord Michael Seaton used that moment to ask her for a dance. She looked to Cy; he nodded and watched as she was swept away into Lord Seaton's arms. Seaton was a good, respectable sort, and Cy did not worry about Ivy learning anything while she danced with him.

A handsome eligible gentleman asked Willow to dance and she was immediately whisked away, leaving Cy alone with the Duchess.

"I must speak with you in private," he said urgently.

She turned her elegantly coifed head, full of mostly gray hair and said, "By all means."

He went to Langley's study, let the Duchess enter before him and closed the door. Without any hesitation he said, "My father's debt has become public knowledge."

"Does Ivy know?" Her eyes widened in horror.

Cy shook his head. "I would like her to remain ignorant."

"She is sure to examine the reason behind your sudden engagement," the Duchess said. "I agree. It is best she know nothing about it."

Sighing in relief that he could count on the Duchess, Cy said, "I think I know the perpetrator who spread the information. I am hoping she only knows about the debt and not about the agreement you and I made."

"She? You think it is a woman?"

"Yes. I think it is Miss Emily Fitzgerald."

The Duchess scoffed. "The girl is not intelligent enough to pull this off, and much too proper to even consider such a thing. Why do you assume it is her?"

Cy's gray eyes went cold. "Only Langley, Fitzgerald and you knew of the debt. It was private and unhandled by creditors."

"What about your solicitor?"

"Crosby has been my solicitor for years and I trust him completely."

"How do you think Miss Fitzgerald found out? Do you think her father told her so she would understand why you broke the engagement?"

"Damned if I know how. I can live with the truth of my father's mistakes surfacing in society. I can even contend with acquaintances refusing to associate with me until they realize I am in fact quite solvent. I will *not* have it found out, however, that the reason I became engaged to Ivy was to clear a debt.

And I sure as hell do not want Ivy to think the marriage wager was all for show."

"Wager, you say?" the Duchess asked, perplexed.

Cy smiled in a moment of remembered brevity. "When she came to Fenton Hill to return the mare I gave her, I asked if she played cards, and we made a wager. If she won, I was supposed to stop courting her and find a 'more worthy female'."

When the Duchess shot him a devilish look, he held up his hands and said, "Her words, not mine. Anyway, if I were to win, she would have to marry me. She pulled the high card, but I managed to convince her to marry me anyway."

"How did you manage that?"

"I asked for a chance to prove to her that she would never regret marrying me. I cannot fail in this." His tone was hard.

"You love my granddaughter."

Cy's gaze was bold and unwavering as he admitted, "Yes."

"I have done right by insisting you two marry," she claimed. "No doubt people will be gossiping and whispering about the debt, but I will do everything in my power to deflect the news from reaching her ears. If she finds out, what should I tell her as well as the rest of the members of society? What are we circulating as a counter rumor?"

"That the debt has been cleared due to some risky business ventures that paid off. If I had never had the debt in the first place, I would be a very wealthy man now. As it stands, my finances are only modest. For the time being, that is."

"You are a wealthy man," the Duchess remarked. "In all the ways that matter."

Grinning wryly, he replied, "Yes, but I plan on having both kinds of wealth. I wish to shower Ivy with anything she could possibly want. She deserves it."

"No one will doubt your genuine feelings. You fought a duel for her," the Duchess pointed out.

"If Ivy finds out the truth, I might have to remind her of that fact."

***

Lieutenant Beaufort threw back the rest of his champagne, steeling himself to approach Miss Fitzgerald and ask her to dance. He was not nervous, not in the least. He loathed this plan, and he silently cursed Langley and Stanton. He had ignored Willow the moment he entered the ballroom, and when he saw the rejected hurt in her eyes, he turned away. To ensure their plot succeeded, he would have to pretend he had eyes for no one except Miss Fitzgerald, even though his gaze strayed to the tall, beautiful blonde across the room.

He sighed and then advanced towards Lord and Lady Fitzgerald. "Good evening. May I dance with your lovely daughter?" he requested. He glanced down at the young woman whose hazel eyes were lit with warm appreciation.

"Absolutely," Lord Fitzgerald said with approval.

Beaufort tried not to sneer, hating that Fitzgerald was sizing up his potential. Everyone knew

Beaufort was the heir to a title, if he could ever be convinced it was in his best interest.

Taking Emily into his arms, Beaufort spun her toward the dance floor, as if they had both rehearsed it a thousand times.

"You are a wonderful dancer," Miss Fitzgerald said with a polite smile.

"Thank you. As are you," Beaufort said. "You are the epitome of what a gentle lady is meant to be." Beaufort tried not to choke on his obsequious words. "Other women simply do not compare to your elegance." He made a point to look directly at Ivy when he said it, hoping Miss Fitzgerald would notice.

"Are you referring to Miss Ivy Sinclair?" she assessed.

"I am. Have you met her?" Beaufort inquired.

Miss Fitzgerald nodded. "I have. Just recently, in fact. She seems…nice."

Beaufort chuckled. "Come now. Let us speak as friends. She has an uncommon background, and now she is engaged to the Earl of Stanton. Surely you do not approve, do you?"

"Perhaps the Earl prefers an un-pedigreed redhead as his future wife."

Beaufort laughed, and Miss Fitzgerald's face glowed. "You have a sparkling wit. May I ask you something a trifle forward?" Beaufort tried to appear seductive.

Her gaze was open, and curious when she nodded.

"There was some talk a while back that you were about to be the next Countess of Stanton. Was the rumor true?"

Miss Fitzgerald thought for a moment. “It is. The Earl had approached my father for my hand in marriage, but when he discovered the Earl’s debt, he refused to let me marry him,” she said with such sincerity that had she been dancing with anyone other than Beaufort, she would have most assuredly been believed.

Beaufort had his answer. He guessed Miss Fitzgerald masked her true nature behind her beautiful façade. She was a vindictive, manipulative shrew, and she had somehow found out about the debt.

Beaufort sighed in mock relief. “Your father is a wise man. Perhaps Miss Sinclair and the Earl deserve each other.”

She chuckled. “Who do you deserve, sir?”

“A woman worth the title of Marchioness,” he said mysteriously, but gave her a look that was meant to entrance her. He tamped down his feelings of disgust when her eyes widened and she greedily licked her lips. The woman wanted a title, not the man behind it.

“I think you could be that woman.”

When she smiled, he felt a surge of victory. They would have the truth and soon.

***

Cy stayed by Ivy’s side throughout the night and refused to let her out his sight. He danced with her more than was proper, and he would not let her dance with anyone he did not know, for fear of improper conversation and Ivy's discovery of the horrid rumor.

When they stood conversing with friends and her family, he leaned down to whisper compliments and witty comments in her ear. Every so often he would catch her gazing at her engagement ring. His fear was measured with excitement. She would be his wife soon.

Wanting a private moment with Ivy, he escorted her onto the balcony. He sat close to her on the marble bench as other couples farther away remained well within eyesight. He took a deep breath of air and was content to look at her. She smiled at him, her face open, guileless. Every emotion registered across her lovely face; he loved that about her.

"Do you realize we are to be married in three weeks?" he asked.

She shook her head. "It seems only yesterday I stepped off the ship from France."

"Do you miss Paris?"

"I miss my mother, but that is not the same thing."

He touched her cheek softly. She came from a humble beginning, and the moment her mother had died, she had nothing. "I want to give you everything, so you never have to worry again."

She turned glowing jade eyes to his and stretched her body up to kiss him. He wanted to run his fingers through her pinned hair, but he stilled his movements and settled for bringing her body close to his for a tender embrace.

When they pulled away from their kiss, Cy gave Ivy a few minutes to catch her breath, and then decided it was time to return to the ballroom. Spending any more time in the dark corner of a balcony with her was dangerous. It took all his willpower not to throw up her skirts and make love to her on the bench.

When they strolled through the double French doors that led back into the ballroom, Cy caught Beaufort's eye who nodded. Cy needed to speak with him, for it was clear Beaufort had information. Not wishing to leave her unattended, Cy escorted Ivy to her grandmother and Willow, and looked to the Duchess.

As if on cue, the old woman feigned, "Oh my, I am positively exhausted. I think it is time to depart this glorious evening, though I hate to pull you and Willow away from the festivities."

"Not at all, Grandmother. If you are tired we shall leave," Ivy said.

"Absolutely," Willow agreed.

"I shall escort you to your carriage," Cy said as he waved down a footman to see to the Cavehill coach.

"You are leaving!" the Countess of Langley pouted in Ivy's direction. "We barely had a chance to speak all evening."

"That is my fault, Lady Langley," Cy said smoothly. "I was occupying most of my fiancée's time."

Ivy turned to the Countess and said, "Thank you for hosting such a lovely party in our honor."

"It was our pleasure, was it not?" She looked to her husband and received a confirmatory nod.

"It was, indeed. Good night ladies," Langley replied.

Cy saw them to their carriage, and then said to Langley, "We should find Beaufort and speak to him now."

They congregated in the library and Langley locked the door so other guests getting lost on their way to the water closet would not disturb them.

Beaufort did not waste any time relaying his thoughts. "I am quite convinced that Miss Fitzgerald is the source of all this unpleasantness." He went on to recount his dance with the chit. "She is a spoiled woman that cares for nothing except a title and the status it will bring her."

Cy cursed and then swallowed a hefty amount of brandy that Langley had given him.

"That still does not explain how she found out," Langley remarked. "Was there anything in writing?"

Cy nodded in affirmation. "Of course. There was a contract, but it was dissolved."

"Perhaps Miss Fitzgerald got her hands on it," Beaufort suggested.

"I am going to speak to Fitzgerald," Cy said.

"And say what?" Langley asked. "Are you going to accuse his daughter of slander?"

Cy stood and went for his coat that he had shrugged off. "I shall do no such thing. I am a gentleman, after all. I will speak plainly and hope the man has some insight."

***

Ivy was in the process of removing the pins from her hair when there was a knock on her bedroom door. She had dismissed her maid, and now she was alone.

"Come in," she called.

Willow stepped into the room, clad in her nightgown and robe. "May I speak with you?" Willow asked.

"By all means." Ivy picked up her brush and began to untangle her curls.

"Lieutenant Beaufort ignored me all evening," Willow said tartly.

"Who is able to ignore you, dear sister?" Ivy teased. "You are beautiful and lively."

"This is serious, Ivy."

"I thought you were not going to settle on him," Ivy said, sobering. "Grandmother disapproves of him."

Shrugging, Willow plopped down on the side of the bed. "I cannot help it. Other men bore me."

"How do you know?"

"Because," Willow answered in exasperation, "I danced with a handful of them tonight. They were all pleasant, but..."

"But not Lieutenant Beaufort," Ivy finished.

Willow nodded morosely. "I do not care that he is untitled. The other night when we danced and spoke, he made me feel like I had known him forever. I did not have to guard my words so closely."

Ivy sighed. It was exactly how she felt about Cy. It seemed her sister was well on her way to becoming infatuated with the handsome lieutenant.

"I saw him dancing with Miss Fitzgerald."

Ivy stopped brushing her hair and shrugged. "It does not mean anything."

Willow sighed in frustration. "He was by her side all evening! And he did not just ignore me when he caught me looking at him, he turned away!"

"You were staring at him?" Willow glared and Ivy went on, "Never mind. It has to be a misunderstanding. The man seemed quite taken with you when you first met."

"You think so?" Willow asked hopefully.

"I know I should echo Grandmother's sentiments, because it would be easier if you set your sights on someone else. Still, the heart wants what it wants." She paused. "Shall I ask Cy about it? Maybe he is privy to Beaufort's thoughts. They are friends."

Willow tossed glossy blonde hair over her shoulder and haughtily replied, "Grandmother is right, he is not worthy. Ask Stanton if you wish, but from this day forward, if I encounter Lieutenant Beaufort in a public setting, I will show him no more favor than any other escort." She swept from the room, head held high with pride, but not with the slightest bit of pretention.

***

Emily Fitzgerald stretched lazily and smiled at the lacy white canopy of her luxurious bed. She wallowed in the crisp white sheets as she thought about the previous night. She started humming as she rang for her maid to help her dress.

"Did you have a good time at the ball, Miss?" her maid asked.

Emily smiled prettily and replied, "It was a lovely ball, Mary."

She was consumed with thoughts of Lieutenant Beaufort, hoping he would call on her soon. Perhaps she would ask her father to invite him to dinner. Maybe then she could manipulate him into telling her of his intentions, and whether or not he wanted to become a marquess.

As Emily walked to the dining room for a late morning breakfast, she asked Cartwright, the butler, "Is my father in his study?"

"No, Miss Emily," Cartwright answered. "Your father went out this morning."

Emily's eyebrows rose. "Where?"

"I do not know," he answered very much out of character. Cartwright knew everything that went on in the household and was paid well for being highly attentive. It was doubtful he did not know the whereabouts of Lord Fitzgerald.

So preoccupied in her own thoughts about becoming a marchioness, she did not challenge his statement. "When he returns, please let me know. I must speak with him at once."

***

"Thank you for coming on short notice," Cy said to Fitzgerald. "I have asked the Count of Langley to join us."

Fitzgerald waved his hand dismissively. "Not at all. Your message was quite vague, sir."

"Did you hear the rumor circulating about my father's debt?" Cy asked without preamble.

Fitzgerald squirmed in his chair, and nodded.

"Only three people knew about it. The Duchess of Cavehill, the Count of Langley and you."

Fitzgerald's voice shook when he spoke, "I did not relay any of our conversations to anyone. I kept that information between us. I am *not* responsible for the rumor, I swear it."

Cy stared at Fitzgerald and then said, "I believe you, but the matter is not resolved. Someone in your household *must* have gotten wind of it. It is the only viable explanation."

Fitzgerald was shocked. "You cannot possibly think my staff would gossip."

"It is not out of the ordinary for servants to whisper about their above stairs employers. It is also well known that servants spread rumors faster than anyone," Langley interjected.

Fitzgerald ran a hand through his hair, which made it stand on end. "My staff is known for their discretion, and we pay them handsomely for it, I assure you," he admitted.

Cy's brow rose as he inquired, "Why would you pay your servants for discretion?"

"My daughter," Fitzgerald explained. "She is my only child. I admit my wife and I have indulged her every whim. She wants for nothing. She has a temper, My Lord." He looked pleadingly at Cy. "Please do not force me to go into more detail."

Langley looked at Fitzgerald and point blankly asked, "Do you think your daughter could be the cause of this?"

Fitzgerald blanched. "I am well aware of her imperfections, but I do not believe her to be malevolent."

"Have you destroyed the evidence of the marriage contract?" Cy asked.

Fitzgerald shook his head and looked embarrassed. "I meant to, but I have not seen to it yet. However, it is in a locked drawer, and I am the only one with a key."

"You will burn the document," Cy said, his voice implacable.

"Absolutely. I will see to it at once."

"I am glad my instincts are correct, Fitzgerald. I believe you can be trusted. Thank you for coming," Cy said, abruptly ending their discussion. He shook Fitzgerald's hand. "I would appreciate your discretion about our conversation today."

Fitzgerald nodded in agreement. "Of course."

When Fitzgerald was gone, Langley looked at Cy and said, "That man is in full denial about his daughter."

Cy agreed. "If our theory is correct, then it is time to utilize Beaufort and his valet."

Langley grinned. "It is too bad you never wanted to work for His Majesty's government. They would have gained a master strategist."

"If this blows up in our faces I may have to join His Majesty's navy in order to escape Ivy's wrath."

"Do not fear. Your fiancée will remain well protected from gossip, thanks to the Duchess." Langley slapped his friend on the back.

"I hope you are right," Cy said resolutely.

***

Two days later, Beaufort perversely thought of doing bodily harm to Stanton and Langley. He was dining with Lord and Lady Fitzgerald and their daughter, Miss Emily and he was ready to jump out the window to make an escape. The girl's insipid eyelash batting and lack of sparkle could not be masked by mere beauty. Beaufort had no idea how Stanton had thought he could marry the bland chit and remain sane. She was driving him daft.

He briefly thought of Miss Willow Sinclair. What was she doing? What would she be like to dine with? Conversation would be lively and intelligent, and her eyes would gleam like sapphires.

Forcing his attention back to the woman at the table, he asked banally, "Do you like to ride, Miss Fitzgerald?"

She shook her pretty blonde head from side to side. "No, sir. I prefer carriage rides through the park." She gazed at him imploringly.

Playing the role of interested suitor, he said, "I would be happy to drive you. Is tomorrow too soon?"

"Tomorrow would be lovely." She smiled at him demurely.

Beaufort thought of the stallion he had seen earlier that day at Southall Market. It was a beautiful animal, unrivaled by any that Beaufort currently owned. He would demand it as a gift from Stanton and Langley as payment for engaging in this charade.

He wondered how this would affect his future courting of Willow. She might never forgive him for his pretend snub, which to her was very real. Before this farce, he had every intention of pursuing her. She never asked about his title; she was interested in him as a man and his experiences. He hated having to stay away from her, but Miss Fitzgerald could not know of his true feelings. Only then would the dull girl give him the information he sought.

Before he left for dinner with the Fitzgeralds, he instructed Sampson, his loyal valet, to find out all he could about who started the rumor.

"I am counting on you, Sampson. I trust you."

Sampson puffed up proudly. "I will not let you down, sir."

Beaufort was eager to find out what Sampson would discover. It was a genius idea to use servants to uncover the truth, and Beaufort was not about to let the opportunity slip away. Most members of the *ton* did not realize their servants knew more than anyone in polite society.

"Cigars and port?" Fitzgerald asked once dinner was over.

Settling in a comfortable leather-backed chair with a fine cigar lit and a glass of port in his hand, Beaufort blew a thick, aromatic smoke ring and said, "Dinner was excellent. You have a wonderful cook."

Fitzgerald beamed and placed his hands on his rotund mid-section. "Thank you. She costs a small fortune to employ, but as you can see we dine well."

The two gentlemen sat in companionable silence before Fitzgerald broached the subject every father had the right to ask of his daughter's suitors.

"What are your intentions?" Fitzgerald's eyes were busy as they assessed Beaufort's passive face.

"I believe Miss Emily possesses many fine qualities that would be suitable in a wife," he said noncommittally.

"*Your* wife?" Fitzgerald pointedly asked.

Beaufort shrugged. "Perhaps. I would like to spend more time with her to see if we would be well matched."

"I want my Emily to be at the pinnacle of society," Fitzgerald said bluntly. "You cannot offer her that kind of status as a mere lieutenant."

"May I speak frankly?" Beaufort asked. "I am in the process of rectifying my relationship with the Marquess of Westonshire, my grandfather. He wishes to make me his heir." Beaufort was surprised that lightening did not strike him for his boldfaced lie. He had no intention of seeking out his grandfather.

"It is no secret that you detest him," Fitzgerald said. "What has changed your mind?"

"I have no desire for the title myself, but if I was to marry a deserving young lady…" He trailed off, casting his possible title like bait on a fishing rod. Fitzgerald swallowed the hook instantly.

"I am glad to hear it, Beaufort. My Emily deserves the best, and you have my blessing to court her."

"Thank you, Lord Fitzgerald. May I ask you a question?"

"Yes."

"Was your daughter engaged to the Earl of Stanton?" Beaufort queried candidly.

"They were betrothed. However, it did not last long and no dowry exchanged hands. The Earl and my daughter agreed they did not suit each other well.

Both parties thought it best to look elsewhere for marriage," Fitzgerald said tactfully.

Beaufort inwardly gave a sigh of relief. Fitzgerald was a gentleman, and Beaufort knew that if there was any talk of his daughter linked to the Earl, Fitzgerald would make sure neither family's reputation would be damaged.

"Excellent. I would hate to think there is any ill will between the two. The Earl and I are acquaintances. It would have been unpleasant to deal with such a situation, but not entirely insurmountable. My cousin Langley is close to the Earl, and every so often I do find myself in Stanton's company."

Fitzgerald nodded. "I understand. However, I thought you and the Earl were more than just mere acquaintances."

"I have dined with the Earl a few times, but being a lieutenant in His Majesty's army keeps me occupied on different parts of the continent throughout the year. Langley is a good host, and tries to make sure I have enough distraction wagering and drinking at White's with some of his closer friends. From time to time I wind up in the presence of the Earl, but we are not close."

"You have allayed all my fears as a father. You are a true gentleman, sir."

Beaufort grinned wryly. "And soon I will be titled."

"A toast then."

"A toast," Beaufort echoed.

"To the future Marquess of Westonshire."

"To your daughter." Beaufort took a sip of port, trying not to choke. He did not know how long he would have to play this game. What if Langley and Stanton made him become engaged to the girl?

Willow would never speak to him again, that was for sure.

***

Long after Beaufort left and the house was settled, Emily snuck downstairs to the kitchen. Cartwright was sitting at an old, scarred table in the kitchen having his customary drink of sherry and reading the newspaper.

"What did you learn, Cartwright?" Emily asked softly.

Cartwright put down his paper, looked at her and smiled. "It seems Lieutenant Beaufort is wondering if you two will be well-matched enough to marry."

Emily bit her lip, pondered the news for a moment and then asked, "Did he say anything about his grandfather?"

Cartwright's eyes were steady as he said, "He is mending his relationship with the old man."

She nodded slowly and stood in silence. She would prefer to be a marchioness than a countess, and the handsome lieutenant was more agreeable than the Earl of Stanton. Beaufort already adored her, clearly. And he was plentiful with his compliments. Why should she waste any more time and thought on the boorish earl, who barely seemed to look at her when he had been in her presence?

"Excellent. Anything else?" Emily pressed.

Cartwright took his time answering.

"Cartwright!" she demanded.

"Beaufort asked about your betrothal to the Earl of Stanton. Your father clarified that you were engaged but *both* parties involved decided they would be ill-suited to each other."

It was not the truth, of course. The Earl had lost interest in her all in thanks to that stupid little nobody, Miss Sinclair. Why was her father protecting Stanton? He had embarrassed Emily, and he deserved to pay the price.

After she returned from Paris, she had decided to find out what happened to make the Earl cry off. She knew where her father kept the key to the only locked drawer of his desk, and there she found all the information she needed to humiliate the Earl of Stanton.

She was glad she had told Cartwright to spread a rumor that her father had been the one to break the betrothal contract after he discovered the late earl's debt. It had shown all of society that her father would not let her marry just *anyone* for the sake of a title. The rumor had saved her reputation; no one knew she had been slighted. What would they think of her if they knew she been chucked out like day old porridge for the illegitimate daughter of a duke?

Emily left the kitchen and padded her way back to her room. She crawled into bed, pulled the covers up to her chin and smiled.

As she slept, she dreamed of her wedding reception to the future Marquess of Westonshire. She twirled in her new husband's arms and out of the corner of her eye, she caught the Earl yelling at his new bride, who had tears streaming down her face.

Chapter XV

London, England

Elizabeth, the Countess of Langley stared at her sleeping two-year-old son. He was face down with his mouth slightly open, his bottom in the air. He slept soundly, without a care in the world. How children managed to sleep in such awkward positions, she would never know.

Her husband quietly entered the nursery and stood by his wife's side. He put his arm around her, and she leaned in close to him.

"Thank you for our son," he whispered.

"You are welcome."

"Would you care for another?" he teased.

"If you are so inclined."

She turned her head for a kiss. He complied, his tongue flicking against hers. She sighed and pulled back. Taking his hand, she led him out of the nursery and down the hall to their room. Marc had already dismissed his waiting valet, and they were alone. His hands immediately went to help loosen the laces of her gown. Slowly bending his head, he kissed her sensitive nape. She pulled away so she could face him.

"You are keeping something from me," she said quietly. "What is it, Marc?"

Her eyes gently probed his face. She did not think for a moment it was another woman. They had sworn fidelity to each other, and she trusted him implicitly.

Marc reached up to touch his wife's cheek. "I could never hide anything from you."

She smiled. "It was a good effort, now explain."

Marc sighed, took her hand and led her to the bed. He sat down next to her and slowly traced the delicate bones of her hand.

"Have you heard the rumor about Stanton's family debt?"

Elizabeth nodded. "I heard it the night of our ball, but I did not think much of it then."

"A few months ago, Stanton was speaking with Lord Fitzgerald about marrying his daughter," Marc said.

Elizabeth's eyebrows rose. "Then the rumor is true?"

"Parts of it. Stanton was engaged to Miss Fitzgerald, but Fitzgerald did not break the betrothal when he found out about the debt."

Elizabeth was captivated by the story. "What happened?"

"It was Stanton who decided not to go forward with the betrothal."

"Why ever not?"

"Because the Duchess of Cavehill had a better offer."

"The Duchess?" Elizabeth exclaimed. "What does she have to do with this?"

"The debt is from Stanton's father. He borrowed money from the late Duke of Cavehill. Stanton inherited his title and the debt."

"He had to repay it to the Duchess herself," Elizabeth murmured.

"Yes, the Duchess asked Stanton to come see her. She had just sent for her two penniless and illegitimate granddaughters. The Duchess told Stanton she would wipe the debt clean if he married Ivy. To sweeten the incentive, she offered him a dowry so his wealth would be restored."

"Good Lord!" Elizabeth breathed. "Does Ivy know?"

Marc shook his head. "No. The Duchess, Stanton and I have been trying to shield her. Stanton does not want her to think he is marrying her to forgo paying a family debt."

Elizabeth bit her lip. "And I am guessing he does not want it known in society either."

Marc grinned at his wife's astuteness. "Stanton does not care if people know of his father's debt, so long as they realize he has the means to repay it. We are trying to whisper in as many ears as possible that Stanton has paid off the debt due to some risky business ventures that were very lucrative. He is now solvent. For all interested parties, that would mean he can marry Ivy of his own free will, and not because he needs money."

Elizabeth's brow furrowed in confusion. "Who started the rumor?"

"You are as smart as any government's secret agent." Marc leaned over to kiss his wife. "We cannot confirm this, but we believe it to be Miss Emily Fitzgerald."

"How?" Elizabeth asked. "Did she know anything of Stanton's situation?"

Marc shook his head back and forth. "She was not apprised of it."

"Then how are you going to discover whether or not she is the cause of it?"

Marc grinned. "We sent Beaufort, disguised as an eligible suitor to visit the Fitzgeralds. We now have reason to think she is hiding behind her servants, and that they were possibly put in charge of circulating the rumor. Beaufort's valet is helping us discover if that is indeed true."

Marc's hand had begun to travel up her nape to the crown of her hair. He slowly removed her hairpins, letting his wife's luxurious brown hair fall in waves across her back.

"Stanton really does care for Ivy," she said as Marc's mouth trailed a stream of kisses up her arm and neck, finally resting on her lips.

"He loves her," Marc admitted.

"Then perhaps he ought to tell her what is going on before someone else does," she said wisely. "It is only a matter of time before she is alone and someone tells her."

Marc made a noncommittal noise in the back of his throat. "I do not wish to talk about this anymore. I am trying to seduce you and you are not being very receptive," he admonished.

"I am sorry," Elizabeth said as she gently pushed him down on the bed and climbed on top of him. "Is this better?"

"Not yet."

She struggled out of her chemise and laid her naked body against his. "Now?"

"Getting warmer," he said with a laugh.

***

Ivy and Willow were walking in Hyde Park, looking for a plush section of grass to set down their picnic basket. When they found an area to their liking, they spread out a large blanket and began to unpack their food.

Ivy had asked the Duchess if she would allow them some respite from normal social activities. Willow had been vacillating between anger and sadness the past few days due to Lieutenant Beaufort's lack of attention, though she would not admit it and hid her despondency from their grandmother. Ivy thought a picnic on one of the rare sunny days in London was just the ticket to distract Willow.

"Good afternoon, Lady Baker. Lord Baker," Ivy greeted the woman and her husband who were strolling towards them.

"It seems everyone is out and about today," Lady Baker said.

"You are correct, my dove," Lord Baker replied absently.

"Everyone?" Willow teased.

"Just about. We recently passed Miss Fitzgerald and Lieutenant Beaufort. They looked like they were having a lovely time of it. Beaufort is escorting her to Lord and Lady Stanhope's masquerade this evening. Will you be in attendance?" Lady Baker chattered on, unaware that Willow had grown unusually quiet when she heard Beaufort was accompanying Miss Fitzgerald.

"Yes," Ivy said.

"Excellent! Good day." Lady Baker tugged on her husband's arm and they continued on their walk.

"Willow—"

"Please, Ivy. I am fine." Willow's lip trembled.

"You are not! How dare he do this? How quickly the man changed his mind. I would love nothing more than to give Lieutenant Beaufort a verbal lashing he will not soon forget!"

"Not on my account, I hope," Willow said pitifully.

Ivy sighed. "Have you decided Beaufort is the one for you?"

Willow shrugged and then nodded. "I think so. I do not know what do to! What am I going to tell Grandmother?"

"Nothing, yet. You have to land him first, and then we will break the news to her. You know, when Cy thought I was receiving undue attention from Lord Caldwell, he swooped in, angry and jealous."

"And got himself entangled in a duel and was nearly killed in the process."

Ivy playfully nudged her sister. "Give Beaufort some competition. Once he sees you flirting outrageously with other men, he will no longer be able to maintain his distance. Stop looking wounded. Shine, Willow. It will drive him daft and bring him back to your side."

Willow's blue eyes were suddenly hopeful. "Do you really think so?"

Ivy nodded. "I do, but Willow, if he does not realize how wonderful you truly are, then he does not deserve your tears."

Willow smiled, grasped her sister's hand and said, "Thank you." Then she changed the subject. "Has anyone seen Caldwell?"

Ivy shook her red curls. "No. It makes Cy quite angry knowing the man is still out there on the loose. He could show up at any moment and cause more trouble."

They were well into their sandwiches when Miss Fitzgerald and Lieutenant Beaufort ambled towards them.

"Smile," Ivy gritted out to Willow, who somehow managed to paste a charming smile onto her face. Ivy did the same.

"Good afternoon," Beaufort said cordially. Miss Fitzgerald's arm was linked through his, but his eyes were on Willow.

"Good afternoon," Ivy replied, feeling a sense of triumph. The man was staring at her sister! "Are you enjoying your outing?"

Miss Fitzgerald fluttered her eyelashes as she looked up at Beaufort, apparently failing to notice his inattentiveness to her. "We are having a marvelous time, are we not?"

Beaufort turned his head and smiled down at Miss Fitzgerald. Was it Ivy's imagination or was his smile strained?

"Marvelous," he agreed.

"Let us not keep you from continuing on your way," Willow said in prim dismissal.

"Are you expecting anyone to join you, or is this a cozy picnic just for two?" Miss Fitzgerald asked snidely.

"My fiancé is joining us soon," Ivy interjected before Willow could snap out a retort. "And perhaps a few of his eligible friends who are quite taken with my sister." Ivy was pleased to note Beaufort's nostril's flaring in suppressed anger. She took it one step further. "She has her hands full trying to juggle all her suitors vying for her attention."

"How does she manage to remember all their names?" Beaufort asked tightly.

Willow smiled brightly, playing along. "I make notecards, and I list all their wonderful attributes."

"Clever," Beaufort snapped.

"Beaufort," Miss Fitzgerald said in annoyance. "Can we be on our way?" She tugged on his arm.

Beaufort inclined his head in farewell.

"You were perfect!" Ivy said.

"Me? What about you?" Willow gushed with a laugh.

"Did you notice Beaufort's reaction when you mentioned notecards? It was priceless!"

"You were right, Ivy. Perhaps Beaufort needs a little reminder that I will not be unattached for long."

"Careful, darling sister. Do not let your head inflate too much, lest it float away."

They laughed and Willow reached for a plum tart. "I am suddenly famished."

"Trapping a suitor works up the appetite," Ivy commented, reaching for her own.

***

Emily slid a bottle of thirty-year-old brandy in front of her butler and asked, "Have you learned anything new?" It was a good thing he was easily bribed. How else was she to learn anything?

"I found out where your father went the other morning," Cartwright said.

Emily shrugged. "He told me he had a business meeting."

Cartwright shook his head. "He went to the Earl of Stanton's home."

"What? Why?"

Cartwright took a long moment to examine one of his fingernails before answering, "It seems the Earl has his suspicions about who started the nasty rumor that is circulating."

Emily's face paled. "Am I a suspect?"

Cartwright shook his head and Emily breathed a sigh of relief. "That is not the most interesting piece of news."

Emily's ears perked up and she leaned forward in her desire for new information. "Go on!"

"The debt was to the Duke of Cavehill. The Duchess told Stanton that if he married her granddaughter, he would not have to repay it."

Emily shook her head as anger raged inside her. "Why would he choose to marry that red-haired *witch* when he could have married me! My dowry would have covered any substantial loan."

Cartwright raised a skeptical eyebrow and said, "The Duchess was willing to offer him a dowry, as well as forgo the debt. Double what your father was giving, you see."

She grinned spitefully and said, "Stanton may have managed to quash the rumor, but I doubt his fiancée will be able to ignore the real reason he is marrying her. I cannot wait for Lord and Lady Stanhope's masquerade this evening!"

Chapter XVI

London, England

Willow was wearing a heavy velvet gown of dark blue that brought out her eyes. The trim was gold, and at her throat was a simple blue ribbon choker that was sure to draw a man's eye to her neckline. Her hair was pulled back into a golden hair net studded with ornate beads. She looked like a lady at court in the reign of King Henry VIII.

"I feel quite unlike myself. I am excited for the masquerade." Willow smiled. In her hand was a decorative gold colored mask on a well-crafted handle that would cover roughly half her face.

"You look perfect. Positively stunning. Lieutenant Beaufort will not be able to stop staring at you."

"Ah, the only goal I have for this evening. Just do not tell Grandmother."

Ivy was dressed in a gown made of champagne colored tulle layers with gold trim. On her feet were a pair of matching ballet slippers with soft soles, and gracing her head was a champagne colored tulle flower with three iridescent pearls at the center. The color of her dress should have washed her out, but it was pale enough that it accentuated the flush of her cheeks and emphasized her loosely pulled back molten waves. Her mask was similar to Willow's.

"Can you believe your wedding is only a week away?" Willow asked.

Ivy shook her head. "No, I cannot."

She was nervous about the wedding though she refused to admit it to anyone. Lately, when Cy came to see her, he was distracted and when she asked him about it, he became closed off, his tone clipped. She hoped he was not having second thoughts about their marriage. She loved him, but she had not professed her feelings, holding out hope that he might feel the same way about her.

"Come, it is time to leave," Ivy said shaking off her thoughts.

"How can you refuse to wear a costume to a masquerade?" Willow demanded of their grandmother when they reached the foyer. The Duchess was holding a black mask not completely ignoring the spirit of the night.

"When you are a duchess, you can do almost anything," she replied imperiously.

Ivy stifled her laughter behind her hand, and Willow's eyes sparkled with merriment.

Lord and Lady Stanhope's ballroom was a sight to behold. The gold chandelier in the center of the room glimmered with hundreds of candles. Along the walls, sconces were well lit, and their light revealed majestic carpentry of the highest craftsmanship.

Ivy had never seen such a crush. Lords and ladies adorned in colorful masks and elaborate costumes graced the dance floor. It was going to be a splendid night. They had just descended the stairs when Cy found them. He was in black formalwear and did not even bother with a mask.

"Apparently, being an earl gives you freedom, too," Willow joked to Ivy.

"You are ravishing this evening," Cy stated as he took Ivy's hand and brought it to his warm lips. "Will you dance with me?"

Without waiting for a reply, Cy glided her towards the dance floor, and only after he had her in his arms did she say, "You realize you did not say one word to my family."

He grinned wryly. "You make me forget myself."

"That is a wonderful compliment."

"I cannot wait to marry you," he admitted fiercely.

"And I cannot wait to become your wife." Her tension evaporated, his words putting her at ease.

Off the dance floor, Willow was busy collecting as many admirers as she could. It was not difficult for she was young, vivacious and witty, not to mention beautiful. Men fell over themselves to fetch her punch and cookies.

"To win a smile from you makes me feel like a knight of old, jousting for my lady's favor," one suitor prattled.

Such was the picture that greeted Beaufort upon his entrance to the ball with Miss Fitzgerald on his arm. His temper frayed upon seeing other men surrounding the woman he wanted. He was on his last nerve. Luckily, he would not have to play Miss Fitzgerald's escort much longer, as there was only one more week until Stanton's wedding. Then Beaufort would be free to pursue Willow again. He did not care if this charade had ruined his chances; he would make her see they were perfect for one another. The object of his thoughts caught his gaze, lowered her mask and then threw him a dazzling smile.

Hot desire pierced him like a spear, and he yearned to shake off Miss Fitzgerald's simpering, wretched claws. He wanted nothing more than to rush to Willow's side and whisk her away from every other man in the room.

"She certainly is playing court," Miss Fitzgerald said contemptuously.

He did not respond to the envious female next to him. "Come, let us dance," he finally said. Anything to take his mind off of Willow and the lust rolling through him.

***

When the waltz ended, Cy escorted Ivy off the dance floor and out into the well-lit garden. Other couples sought solitude, whispering in far off shadows, but Ivy and Cy did not stray too far from the welcoming light of the ballroom.

"Would you care for some champagne?" he asked as he leaned close to Ivy's ear. His warm breath swept across her skin and caused her to shiver. She nodded and smiled at him.

"Your smallest wish is my command," he teased.

She watched him walk away until he disappeared from sight into the throng of guests. Ivy turned around and surveyed the immaculately groomed gardens, loving the tall, hedged maze. She could imagine stolen moments alone with Cy in the labyrinth, and she quivered in delight.

She was alone for less than a minute when she heard a smooth voice from behind her purr, "May I say how delectable you look this evening?"

She knew the owner of the voice, and it made her skin crawl.

Lord Brandon Caldwell.

She turned slowly, the torchlight of the garden revealing half his face. The other half was in shadow, but no amount of darkness could conceal his blatant perusal of her form.

The man had disappeared for weeks after he nearly killed Cy, and now he had reappeared at a social event as if nothing had transpired. Only a vile man would wait until a woman was alone and then have the gall to pounce, but Caldwell was like a weak lion, afraid to go in for the kill until there was no competition.

Without thinking, Ivy flew at him and managed a swift kick to his shin, though her slipper did little damage. She cursed the soft sole. She pounded him with her ineffectual fists that he quickly trapped in his larger hands.

She raged verbally instead. "How dare you! You deceitful coward! You almost killed him, and then you ran away you…you…*evil snake*!"

Something dark moved in Caldwell's blue eyes, and at once Ivy was afraid, her anger vanishing instantly. She tried to tug her hands out of his, but he gripped them tighter.

"Such loathsome language from such a beautiful lady."

She prayed for Cy to return. "Why you came back, I will never know. You should have stayed away. Cy will surely kill you when he sees you."

Caldwell gazed at her, unperturbed by her threat. "I am surprised Stanton would leave you alone for even a moment."

"He is procuring me a glass of champagne."

Caldwell smiled, but it was filled with mocking irreverence. "Ah yes, of course. No doubt to toast your impending nuptials. Though I doubt you will be in such a celebratory mood once I share a bit of information with you."

"Nothing you can say will provoke me." She attempted to shake him off again, but his grasp was unyielding. He was hurting her, but she refused to cry out.

"Care to know the *true* reason the Earl of Stanton broke his engagement to Miss Fitzgerald?" he taunted.

Despite herself, she was intrigued, and her curiosity surpassed her fear. Unable to hide her interest, she asked, "What do you know about it?"

"It is fascinating what one can uncover regarding someone like Stanton, who just happens to be the talk of the town."

"Spare me the dramatics, please," Ivy spat.

"So willful," he murmured and licked his lips lasciviously.

Her stomach rolled in distaste.

"Miss Fitzgerald has been gracious enough to share some information with me. It seems the Earl's father incurred a debt. Your fiancé and the Duchess struck a deal. If he marries you, you see, he will not have to pay back the *astronomical* debt. Rumor has it, it is so large it would financially cripple almost anyone."

The blood drained from her face. "I do not believe you," Ivy whispered though her words lacked conviction. She tried to reject the idea, but needles of uncertainty pierced her.

"No? Then perhaps we should seek out Miss Fitzgerald so you may hear the words from her own lips."

"Miss Fitzgerald is upset because Stanton broke their engagement, and she had her heart set on becoming a countess. I would not believe anything she says."

"Then perhaps you will believe me when I tell you the Duchess gave Stanton a dowry worth the amount of the debt. Not only did Stanton not have to repay it, but he also became rich from his engagement to you! The Earl was nearly destitute!"

She could no longer disregard Caldwell's words. They were hurtful, and she knew he was trying to rile her, but they rang of truth. She loved a man who did not love her; her fear of becoming her mother was obsolete. Ivy was even more pathetic.

The voices from the party were nothing more than a soft hum in the background. Ivy was so obsessed with her thoughts that she did not notice Caldwell pulling her deep into the garden maze. When she realized what he was doing, she dug her heels into the ground, but her shoes were soft and flat, and she lost them in the struggle.

How could she have forgotten about Caldwell's sordid nature? She had to get away from him, or die trying! She began to scream, uncaring who heard, only wishing that someone would find her before it was too late. She would not hope it would be Cy; he did not care about her at all. It had been an act on his part. Her tortured heart twisted in confused agony, and beat harder every second as fear of what Caldwell might do to her began to sink in. The view of Stanhope manor had long disappeared, as well as the warm sight of torchlight.

But she was no match for Caldwell's determined strength. While she fought, he placed an arm around her body like an iron manacle, and clamped his other hand over her mouth. She sank her teeth into his meaty palm. Caldwell cursed and snatched his hand free. The arm he had around her tightened fiercely, cutting off her ability to breathe, or scream for help.

"You will regret that," he promised menacingly.

"Why are you doing this? What will you gain by hurting me?" Her words came in pants, her breathing labored, her voice shallow and strained.

"Hurt you?" he said with a touch of humor. "What makes you think I would hurt you? You are a glorious creature."

Her pulse raced, a solid drumming in her chest. She realized his intentions. A ripple of fear coursed through every vein in her body, and she remembered what Cy had said about Caldwell's fiendish pleasure in abusing women.

"Must you really ask why I have drawn you away from the ballroom?" Caldwell asked in a seductive whisper. "I want to shower you with passion and feel your sweet body press against mine."

His tone and words sent a jolt of terror down her spine. She began to shake.

Mistaking her trembling as a sign of pleasure, he chuckled and roughly turned her towards him so that her face was mere inches from his. With a quirk of his lips, he began to lower his head.

***

"Get away from her," Cy commanded, stepping out from behind the bushes, hot rage erupting in him like a volcano. The bastard had his hands all over Ivy's soft, tender skin. Her eyes were wide in her pale face while she was busy shooting Cy silent accusations. *She knows, then, about it all,* he realized resolutely.

He wanted nothing more than to take her into his arms and soothe the pain he had caused her, but for the moment, he needed to focus on the cowardly scoundrel holding the woman he loved.

Ivy's gold mask dangled from Cy's fingers. He had returned to the garden with two glasses of champagne only to find Ivy gone, her mask scattered on the ground. He dropped the flutes, and they crashed to the stone, as he dashed deeper into the garden.

"Why are you holding my fiancée?" Cy asked, his voice cold and distant, like a predator ready to strike.

"She is where she wants to be, Stanton," Caldwell taunted. His arms tightened around her ribs when Ivy gasped. "The lady was merely seeking the solace of my embrace when she discovered your true motives for marrying her."

"Let her go, Caldwell. This is between you and me."

Caldwell pretended he had not heard the demand. Instead, he reached up to caress the back of Ivy's elegant neck.

Reacting violently, Cy dropped the gold mask and lunged for Caldwell. In a spineless act, Caldwell attempted to shove Ivy in front of him to deflect Cy's charge, but all he managed to do was lose his hold on her. Ivy fell roughly into the dirt, collapsing with a cry of distress.

Cy's fist connected with Caldwell's nose, but the sound of breaking cartilage and the sight of spurting blood was not enough satisfaction for him. He had been pushed beyond reason, and his deepest instincts to protect the woman he loved roared to life. He braced firmly and prepared to strike again.

Through his haze of pain and anger, Caldwell counterattacked. It took Cy by surprise, and both men fell to the ground in a heap of flying fists and curses. Cy was on his back, and Caldwell rose like a venomous serpent ready to assail its prey. With one hand on Cy's throat, Caldwell pulled back to punch him in the face, but when his fist came crashing down, Cy moved. Caldwell's knuckles smashed into the unyielding dirt below them.

Caldwell howled when Cy took the opportunity to slam his elbow into the man's already broken nose. The second strike was too much for him to bear, and he collapsed in a pitiful heap, teary-eyed and writhing in pain.

Standing up, Cy finally spared a look in Ivy's direction. She had risen from the ground. Dirt smudged her face and covered her delicate tulle dress.

"Ivy, are you hurt. Did that bastard harm you?" Cy walked towards her and reached out to touch her cheek, but she recoiled, her green eyes glistening with unshed tears.

"No more than you hurt me. Did you and my grandmother strike a bargain? Is what Miss Fitzgerald told Caldwell true?"

Cy's jaw clenched. He had been correct about Miss Fitzgerald being the cause of the rumor, but he felt no satisfaction as he responded, "It has been a long night, Ivy. Let us leave. I will explain everything."

She shook her head adamantly. "No, I will not go anywhere with you. You lied to me."

Before Cy could reply, Beaufort rounded the bend of the maze and stopped. "There you two are. You have been gone a long time. The Duchess had an inkling you two were together." He looked at Ivy, wondering why she looked so disheveled.

"Did I interrupt something?" Beaufort asked looking back and forth between a Cy who was grim, and Ivy who was clearly distressed. Caldwell let out a moan that alerted Beaufort to his presence. He was still wriggling like a worm, and unable to get up.

"What is going on? Caldwell is back?" Beaufort demanded.

"Yes, and he informed me of the truth behind Cy's reason for marrying me. His only reason," she clarified.

Cringing as the words parted from her lips, Cy turned to Beaufort and said, "Ivy is not feeling well and has to leave. We will be taking Her Grace's carriage to my townhouse." He paused thoughtfully. "Caldwell has a desire to see America. Find Langley and escort Caldwell to the docks." He looked meaningfully at his friend.

"I understand. No one will be the wiser to your departure…or his," Beaufort promised as he looked at Caldwell scathingly.

With all due haste, Cy grabbed Ivy's hand and ran off into the night.

***

"Where is he taking my sister?" a musical voice asked from behind Beaufort. He turned, and his breath left his body. Willow was bathed silver in moonlight, but at the moment he did not have time to be distracted by her beauty.

"You should not have followed me," he admonished.

She glared at Beaufort and crossed her arms over her chest. He wanted nothing more than to drag her off into the night just like Stanton had done with Ivy.

Willow's gaze went to Caldwell. "Is that who I think it is?" she asked in shock.

"It is. Miss Sinclair, I must enlist your aid. Will you find Lord Langley immediately?" She nodded, and without hesitation, ran to find the Count of Langley while Beaufort stood guard.

Moments later she returned with the Count. Caldwell was attempting get up off the ground, but Langley walked over to Caldwell and kicked him in the groin. The man groaned in pain and rolled over, retching expensive champagne.

"Stanton suggested Caldwell see America," Beaufort explained as he took in Caldwell's pitiful form.

"A sound plan. I will have my driver meet us in back with the carriage." Langley left quickly and Willow and Beaufort were alone.

"Are you courting Miss Fitzgerald?" Willow blurted out.

"You do not know how to prioritize, do you?" Beaufort asked wryly.

"Are you?" Willow pressed.

Beaufort shook his head and took a step towards her. "No. I am courting you."

"You have not come to call," Willow pointed out haughtily. "And I am not even sure I want you courting me. You seem very indecisive when it comes to your feelings. I have plenty of other suitors who—"

Wrapping his arms around her, he silenced her protest with his lips. When Beaufort lifted his head, Willow went right on talking like nothing had occurred.

"As I was saying, I have plenty of other suitors who—"

He growled like a bear. "You will have no other suitors besides me." He kissed her again, thoroughly. He was pleased to see her eyes were glazed with both desire and anger when he ended their kiss. "Shall we continue with this discussion about your other suitors? Would you like to tell them to stop calling, or should I?"

Willow did not reply as Langley returned with the Duchess and his wife in tow. Willow hastily attempted to step out of Beaufort's arms, but he tightened his hold, refusing to let her go.

"Langley and I will take Caldwell to the docks," Beaufort explained. "The rest of you will take Stanton's carriage to his townhouse. We will congregate there."

"Where are Ivy and Stanton?" the Duchess asked as she peered at her other granddaughter.

It was Beaufort who answered, "Gone, they left in your carriage, Your Grace. Miss Sinclair discovered the truth behind their engagement."

"Oh, dear," the Countess said.

"She is not the only one who knows," the Duchess remarked dispassionately. "It seems it is all over the ballroom. The guests are also speculating on Ivy's current whereabouts."

Langley started to drag Caldwell away and then glared at his cousin. "Do you think you can let go of Miss Sinclair long enough to help me?"

Grumbling, Beaufort released Willow and did as requested.

"We will have a long talk about your behavior very soon, young lady," the Duchess admonished.

"We have a crisis on our hands. You must learn to prioritize, Grandmother," Willow remarked, causing Beaufort to shout with laughter.

***

"Let go!" Ivy yelled.

"No," Cy said implacably as he continued to drag her towards the Duchess's carriage.

"Where are you taking me?"

"To my townhouse where you are going to listen to me so I can explain myself."

She tried to twist free. "I do not need or want an explanation. You do not wish to marry me. I only wish I knew this before I fell in love with you!" she shouted, nearly hysterical.

Cy did not react to her admission that she was in love with him. Instead, he turned to her and hoisted her over his shoulder so she could not escape.

"How—how dare you!" she fumed as she pummeled his back with her tiny fists.

He squeezed her leg through her skirts. "Quiet, Ivy. I do not want your reputation ruined."

"You should have thought of that before!"

After a long, tense carriage ride, they finally reached Cy's townhouse.

"I am not going in there with you," she stated.

Sighing, Cy hauled her out of the carriage and hoisted her back onto his shoulder. The butler opened the door and gaped at his master, who clearly looked as though he had been rolling around in the dirt. The servant's gaze widened when he realized Cy was carrying a cursing and bedraggled woman over his shoulder.

"We will be in the drawing room. Do not disturb us."

Once they were alone, Cy set Ivy down. She stared in mute defiance as he went to the liquor cart and poured two overly full glasses of brandy. He gave her one and said with grim humor, "Please wait until after my explanation before you throw this in my face."

"I am a fool," she whispered even as she took the glass. Her skin crawled as she thought of Caldwell's hands on her. Ivy wanted to scrub away every trace of him.

"Take a sip. It will steady your nerves."

She frowned, but did as he suggested. The brandy burned a trail down her throat and then curled in a warm pool at the bottom of her belly, and she felt calmer.

"My father was a notorious gambler," Cy began. "Heavily in debt, he mortgaged his lands and was about to lose Fenton Hill. He approached the Duke of Cavehill for a loan. He died before ever paying it back, and it fell to me. Slowly, I managed to save my properties, invest in wise business ventures, and would have been able to restore my former wealth, except for the crippling debt. I only planned to marry Miss Fitzgerald for her dowry. It would have paid the debt in full, and I would finally start turning a profit.

"Your grandmother requested a meeting and suggested the arrangement between us. I only agreed *after* I met you. I broke off the engagement to Miss Fitzgerald immediately.

"If I had not wanted you, Ivy, I would have married Miss Fitzgerald and been done with it, but you walked into the drawing room and I knew I had to be with you. You made my blood heat from a mere look."

She shivered from the possessive longing in his voice and whispered brokenly, "You desired me, but you do not care for me, not even now."

Achingly, he said, "At first it was just desire, and yes, a hunger to have you, but we grew closer. I fought a duel for you, Ivy. How can you doubt the sincerity of my feelings?"

Ivy shook her head as tears began to fall down her rosy pink cheeks. "I want to believe you."

"Remember the card wager? I could have let you walk out the door, but I knew I had to convince you to marry me." He moved towards her but did not take her into his arms.

"When the truth about my father's pitiful legacy surfaced, I became distant, trying to discover the truth. Langley, Beaufort and I had a hunch Miss Fitzgerald was the cause of the rumor which is why Beaufort appeared to be courting her. We needed him to get close to her for information. I tried to shelter you, and it caused more damage than if I had just been honest. You may not believe me, Ivy, but I love you."

His hand slowly came up to caress her cheek, and she looked into steely gray eyes naked with longing and love.

"Please tell me I have not lost you." He cradled her face in his hands. "I have courted you for months, punched Caldwell in the face twice, and almost died in a duel defending your honor. What else can I *possibly* do to prove to you that I am in love with you?"

"Why *are* you in love with me?" she whispered.

"I will make you a list of reasons later," he said just before his mouth covered hers.

She kissed him back, her arms twining around his neck, and she pressed against him. His hands slid lower, and he pulled her so she was cradled against the junction of his thighs. His fingers removed the tulle flower in her hair, and the pins that held her luscious waves back from her face. Her silky tresses flowed over his hands as he cupped her head and continued the onslaught of her lips.

Her tongue touched his and the kiss deepened. Pushing his hips against her, he growled his approval at her boldness. She grew more confident as the passionate kiss continued.

Ivy reached for his cravat and began to untie it. His gray eyes were dark with desire as he watched her. She began to undo the top buttons of his shirt, and when the sensitive skin of his throat was exposed, she leaned over and kissed it with warm, rosy lips.

His fingers wove through her hair, and gently pulled her head back. She was glad that he was becoming the aggressor again. She liked when he took charge, for it made her feel like a wild, uninhibited woman. It was primal.

Backing her up against the closed door, Cy teased apart the layers of tulle that covered her body, his fingers grazing silken skin.

"I want to be inside you," he whispered harshly.

"Yes," she moaned, a fresh surge of lust flowing through her veins.

Cy pulled down the straps of her dress to reveal pink nipples. She shivered under his gaze, just as he bent to take one perfect bud into his mouth. She gasped, and leaned into him as she grabbed his head to keep her balance.

"Cy," she whispered, her voice a mixture of awe and desire.

"I know, love," he said gruffly.

He slowly moved them away from the door and lowered her to the carpet, ridding himself of his shirt. The candlelight showed a perfectly formed, muscular chest, and Ivy yearned to stroke him.

"Touch me," he pleaded.

She complied and reached out to put her hand on his thundering heart. His gray eyes were liquid silver and his gaze was burning her with desire. She pressed kisses all over his chest, and when her tongue touched his nipple, he cried out.

"Should we move to a bed?" he gasped.

"Why?" she murmured huskily. Her hand trailed lower, covering the bulge in his tight trousers.

"Speak now or forever hold your peace," he mumbled. "I want to see you, feel you." He divested himself of the rest of his clothing and helped her out her dress. "I have never seen such perfection." He traced a silky breast and his thumb brushed an erect nipple. Her magnolia flesh fit in his hands perfectly, and she stared at him with emerald eyes full of love.

Cy leaned over and covered her body with his, and she enjoyed his rippling hard muscles pressing against her sensitive skin. He kissed the side of her neck as his hand skimmed her body and settled on her curly red mound. He began to stroke the inside of her thigh and inched closer to her silky, wet center.

"I want to make you scream with pleasure," he whispered against her mouth.

"Cy," she breathed as he slowly inserted a finger into her warmth, gasping at his tender invasion. He began to move his finger back and forth. She thrashed around and grabbed his neck as she pulled herself closer.

"Oh God," she moaned as he slid another finger into her, tantalizing her core, making her ravenous with need.

Removing his fingers, he nudged her legs farther apart seeking her moist entrance with his straining manhood. "I cannot wait any longer."

"Please." She begged for something she knew not.

"It will hurt."

"I trust you."

When he eased into her body, she stretched to accommodate his size. She was hot, feverish. She was scorched from the inside out. He thrust forward with love and lust, and she cried out in pain.

"I am sorry," Cy said in a labored voice.

She sobbed in discomfort, and Cy pressed tender kisses along her hairline and jaw; it was a paltry distraction. When her cries turned to whimpers, he began to move. Moans of her pleasure echoed off the drawing room walls. He was fanning the flames of her desire, pitching her forward until she was bathed in ecstasy, the pain of his entrance a dim memory.

Cy's brow beaded with perspiration as he maintained steady strokes. Her legs opened wider, taking his shaft in deeper, welcoming him, bringing him home.

As he thrust, she knew she was on the brink of exploding. She screamed, the culmination too much for her to stay quiet. Gripping him tightly, she rode out the waves of pleasure until they were small eddies. With a shout, Cy gave in to his own release, thrusting hard, burying himself deep inside her.

"I had no idea it could be that way," she breathed in awe.

"I did. From the first moment I saw you."

"Is this the true reason you wanted to marry me?" she teased. She felt warm, sated; her insides gooey like melted chocolate.

Leaning up, he looked into her eyes and cradled her cheeks in his hands. "Do you forgive me? I should have confided in you. It is a mistake I will never make again."

She tenderly stared at his impassioned face. She was nothing like her mother, she realized. She had not fallen in love with a man who could only give part of himself to her. Cy gave her everything he was, and the realization of it was so beautiful she nearly cried.

"You wanted to protect me. I see that now." She burrowed close to him and he wrapped his strong arms around her.

There was a knock on the door interrupting their intimate moment.

"We are occupied!" Cy yelled out, thinking it was a footman or a maid.

Ivy stifled a giggle.

"My Lord, it is the Duchess of Cavehill and…company," the harassed butler said through the closed door.

"Oh God!" Ivy whispered, feeling embarrassment climb up her cheeks. "They are going to know!"

"Hush," he said, even though his own face suffused with color. They flew into action. "Give us five minutes, and show them to the library," Cy called to the butler. He threw on his clothes and helped Ivy with her dress, but they both knew they could never restore order to her hair.

He gave her one last lingering kiss, clasped her hand and opened the door. They walked down the hallway to library where the Duchess, Willow, Beaufort and the Count and Countess of Langley were all seated, waiting for them.

Ivy's face heated when she saw her grandmother taking in her appearance. The woman clamped her mouth shut even though her eyes shined with knowledge. Seating Ivy in the chair behind his desk, Cy moved to stand next to her.

"Caldwell?" he asked getting down to the matter at hand.

"Bound and gagged and on his way to America," Langley said with a smile.

"It is only half of what he deserves," Willow said with disdain.

"Agreed," Cy said. "I would have liked to break one of his legs."

Everyone murmured agreement at his sentiment.

"At least he is gone," Ivy said.

Cy looked at the Duchess. "I prefer if Ivy and I did not have to wait a week for the wedding."

"That may be our best course of action. Ivy's absence from the ball was duly noted." The Duchess sniffed.

"Caldwell dragged Ivy into the garden maze. If that bastard has ruined her reputation—" Ivy placed a hand on Cy's arm to calm him down. He grabbed her hand and squeezed it.

"If only people assumed you two had run off into the night…" The Duchess trailed off thoughtfully and then looked at Willow and Beaufort. "It is no secret the both of you were there together, as well. People will talk."

"Beaufort and I will get married," Willow blurted out.

The Duchess gasped in shock. "Willow!"

Ignoring her grandmother and everyone else in the library, she looked at Beaufort. "You are going to ask me to marry you, are you not?" she demanded.

Beaufort gave a long-suffering sigh. "I suppose. It would be the honorable thing to do."

"I am waiting," Willow pressed.

"Would you like me to get down on one knee?" he asked in exasperation.

"You may remain seated," Willow replied magnanimously.

"Thank you. I would have preferred to do this in private, you know."

"Do get on with it, man," Cy said. "We have other things to take care of tonight. Like procuring a last minute marriage license."

"Hush, this is a very important moment," Ivy chastised.

Beaufort quirked an eyebrow in wry amusement. "Yes, I am so glad to have an audience when I ask for Miss Sinclair's hand in marriage."

"Under the circumstances, Beaufort, I do believe you may call me Willow." She smiled beautifully.

"Let us get out the champagne to celebrate," the Countess of Langley said.

Everyone started conversing and chattering away. Beaufort leaned over and whispered in Willow's ear, "I did not technically ask you to marry me, yet."

"Foregone conclusion, is it not?" she asked.

He grinned. "I suppose so.

"You are going to make me very happy," she predicted.

Shouting with laughter, Beaufort said, "As if you would settle for anything less."

Chapter XVII

London, England

Cy smiled at his wife of six hours who was sitting next to him in the carriage. At the moment, she was trailing a seductive path with her fingertips down his thigh.

"Careful, darling. I do not have time to properly satisfy you before we reach our destination."

She chuckled. "Beaufort's plan is brilliant."

"He is the Earl of Bedford, now."

"I had forgotten," Ivy said absently.

"There has been a lot of commotion in the past twenty four hours."

"Caldwell is America bound, the Marquess of Westonshire reinstated Bedford as his heir, Bedford and my sister became engaged, and I got into a yelling match with Grandmother."

"You forgot the most important part," Cy said softly. "We got married."

"So we did."

"Tell me more about this fight you had with the Duchess."

"After we left your townhouse and returned home, I confronted her."

"It was not her fault, Ivy."

"You enlisted her aid to keep the truth a secret from me."

"It was for your own good."

She looked at him. "Do you want to start another fight?"

"The last one ended quite nicely. You would up naked in my arms," he remarked dryly. "Go on."

Sighing, she continued. "She did not apologize for her high-handedness."

"She is a duchess."

"She used the exact same excuse!" Ivy snorted with laughter. "She claimed to know how well we would suit one another."

"Are you upset by the outcome, my dear?"

"Not in the least," Ivy replied breezily.

"Is everything resolved between you?"

"Yes."

"Good."

"Does everyone in society already know we were married?" Ivy inquired.

"News travels quickly, especially among the servants," Cy quipped. "They will assume we are incurable romantics who simply could not wait any longer to be married."

"When I tell them about the ballet studio you had commissioned as a wedding gift, everyone will believe it." She looked at him tenderly. "Thank you. It is lovely."

He kissed her palm. "A lovely gift for a lovely woman."

Last night, after celebrating Bedford and Willow's engagement, Cy stole Ivy away for a quick moment so he could show her what had been built for her. The studio was large, and long mirrors covered every wall. Wooden bars were placed on two sides of the room and a pianoforte graced one corner. It brought tears to Ivy's eyes when she realized how much time and effort had gone into such a thoughtful gift for her. If Cy had not already professed his love, she would know how he felt from the gift.

"It made Grandmother angry since she believed I had given up ballet long ago."

"I never want you to stop practicing. I love who you are, Ivy. Will you dance for me?" His voice was deep with desire as he pressed a kiss to her lips. It was meant to be quick and chaste, but Cy apparently had other ideas.

"To hell with time," he muttered pulling away from her. He sank to the floor of the carriage.

"What are you doing?" she demanded, as he reached for her skirt.

"The only thing I can, darling. I have to touch you."

Her breath hitched in her throat when he pulled up her skirts, pushing apart her drawers. His finger danced across her skin, and she felt herself grow heavy and wet between her legs. She heard him hum in pleasure.

Bending his head, he glided his tongue across her swollen bud, and she cried out.

"Hush, love, or passersby will know what we are doing." He grinned devilishly, returning his attention to her.

Stifling a cry, she came, saying his name over and over again.

He tugged down her skirts and took his place on the plush seat next to her, brushing at his pants to make sure they were dust free. The carriage came to a halt.

"Do I look presentable?" she asked breathlessly.

Chuckling, he stroked her face. "Your cheeks are flushed and your eyes are sparkling. You look like a fallen angel."

She sighed. "If you weary of tending to business investments, you should seriously consider becoming a poet. You say the most beautiful things to me."

"This is only a small taste of the pleasure I will give you. Tonight will be very fulfilling," he whispered hotly, reaching for the door of the carriage.

The moment Cy and Ivy were announced as the Earl and Countess of Stanton, the gossiping nobles stopped in mid-conversation to stare at them. The whispers began almost immediately. Cy took her hand as they approached their hosts, a middle-aged couple that was at the pinnacle of society.

The Duke of Bellington slapped Cy on the back firmly and said, "Congratulations, my boy. Took matters into your own hands, did you? Could not wait even a week?" He elbowed Cy playfully, while the Duchess of Bellington threw him a look.

"I would have loved to be at the wedding," the Duchess said wistfully.

"And we would have loved to have had you there, Your Grace," Ivy said graciously, "but I am afraid when one is in love, even a week seems too long to wait!"

The Duchess sighed. "You both are absolutely precious."

"Careful, Stanton," the Duke said to Cy. "One more romantic gesture like that and you will make the rest of us married chaps look bad."

Cy smiled and shrugged. Ivy smiled gorgeously. "My husband is such a thoughtful man. Did I tell you what he gave me for a wedding present? He had a ballet studio built just for me! He knows I love to practice!"

The Duke shook his head. "Ruined. You have absolutely ruined the rest of us."

"I am sorry, sir," Cy said, not looking at all contrite.

They paused in conversation to welcome the arrival of the Duchess of Cavehill and the Langleys. Willow, who was on the arm of her fiancé, the Earl of Bedford, the newly made heir to the Marquess of Westonshire, trailed behind them. The Marquess completed their entourage.

The elderly man carried an elegant cane, but it was all for show as his carriage was still erect. When his grandson had contacted him late the previous evening, the Marquess agreed to make him his heir on the condition that Bedford leave the military and stay close to him. They had lost too many years already.

The aging Marquess was busy engaging the Duchess of Cavehill in conversation, and she was doing her best to pretend she was not enjoying his attention. Lord and Lady Fitzgerald along with their daughter, approached their group.

Lord Fitzgerald said, "Congratulations on your wedding, Stanton."

"Whatever are you going to do with the wedding preparations already in place?" Lady Fitzgerald asked.

The Duchess of Cavehill smiled smugly. "My other granddaughter, Miss Willow Sinclair, will marry the Marquess of Westonshire's heir, the Earl of Bedford, on that day."

Willow turned to Miss Fitzgerald and smiled sweetly, "Will you be able to attend?"

Before the chit was able to reply, her father spoke up, "No, afraid not. My daughter is going to spend some time in Brussels with her relatives." He shot his daughter a meaningful look.

"I am looking forward to seeing my extended family," Miss Fitzgerald intoned blandly, though her face colored in anger.

"Yes," Fitzgerald nodded. "We expect her to make a wonderful match abroad."

Ivy was glad to know that Miss Fitzgerald would be nowhere near London for a long period of time, and with Caldwell bound for America, their lives were dangerously close to perfection.

"The look on Miss Fitzgerald's face was priceless," Willow remarked when the Fitzgeralds had moved along.

"She was quite unable to conceal her annoyance at having another bachelor snatched from under her nose," Stanton agreed with a smile. "By another Sinclair woman, no doubt."

Willow smiled boldly in Bedford's direction. "Can you believe we are getting married in a week?"

"Six days, actually," Bedford corrected.

"To think," Willow said with a shake of her head, "My grandmother pretended she did not approve of you."

"I only knew that would make you want him more," her grandmother replied, overhearing their conversation. "And that you would fight for him."

Willow blushed.

"You did not approve of my grandson?" the Marquess demanded brusquely. "He is a fine catch!"

"Of course he is," the Duchess soothed. "I knew they would be perfect for one another, and to ensure they realized it, I had to give my granddaughter an obstacle to overcome."

"You gave me your own obstacle," Willow said to Bedford. "Pretending to court Miss Fitzgerald made me miserable."

"It made me miserable as well," Bedford said, causing everyone to laugh.

Langley grabbed his wife's hand and kissed it, and said, "Let us dance."

"Langley! Whatever has come over you? You loath dancing!" the Countess jested.

"I am in a celebratory mood," he said.

"Why is that?" Ivy inquired.

"Shall we tell them?" Langley whispered to his wife.

"In eight months, Malcolm will have a little brother or sister," the Countess of Langley said shyly.

When the three couples had taken to the dance floor, the Duchess looked at her granddaughters with pride in her eyes. They had brought laughter and joy back into her home; she was no longer alone or lonely. She never could have guessed that her son's indiscretions would give her a family she was proud of. Soon, Ivy and Willow would have children, and the thought of hearing soft, childish giggles filled her with delight. Through the years, she would watch their family grow.

She had done well for them.

Her gaze lingered on Ivy who looked like a young version of the Duchess. Ivy stared adoringly into her new husband's eyes, the devotion and love she felt clearly evident for all to see. The Duchess's heart beat once again with the remembrance of excitement, youth and love.

Yes, she had done well for them.

***

The smell of sea and fish assaulted Caldwell's senses. He attempted to move, but his body ached in protest. As he regained full consciousness, he remembered his fight with Stanton. It had ended with Caldwell squirming on the ground in pain.

Slowly, he opened his eyes. He nearly screamed at his surroundings, but his throat was too dry, and no sound came out. A swarthy, stout man with a grizzly beard leaned over him, silhouetted by the rising sun. The scent of stale sweat, putrid deck wood and brine was overwhelming, and Caldwell wanted to turn his head and retch. The rocking of the sailing ship made his broken nose and bruised body throb.

The burly pirate cackled, showing decaying teeth. "Finally awake, are ye?"

"Where am I?" Caldwell asked, licking dry, cracked lips.

"Aboard the mighty *Sea Serpent*, bound fer America."

Caldwell paled and tried to stand up. "But…how did I get here?" His head was fuzzy and his stomach rolled as the ship swayed on choppy waves.

His new companion shrugged. “Two men carried ye aboard last night with instructions te work ye hard an’ make sure ye earn ye keep. They brought with ’em a vast purse fer the captain to keep ye onboard.”

A sheen of sweat beaded Caldwell’s forehead, and he felt shaky. He had never done a hard day’s work in his life, and now he was on a ship in the middle of the sea being carried further and further away from his home. He figured at best it would take a month to get to America if the weather was favorable, and another to return.

“When do we head back to England?” Caldwell gripped the wooden rail without thinking and instantly gasped in pain due to the shattered bones in his swollen hand.

“A year. Maybe two,” the man said. “We aren’t *just* goin’ te America. Now that yer awake, grab that bucket an’ brush. The deck needs a good scrubbin’. If ye shirk yer duties, the captain has no qualms about throwin’ ye overboard an’ lettin’ the sharks take a bite out o’ ye.” The strapping sailor eyed Caldwell, taking in his broken nose, ruined hand, and grayish face. “An’ from the looks of ye, I doubt ye’d be able te swim three feet before the sharks get ye...”

Caldwell closed his eyes. *This has to be a nightmare*, he thought.

He heard scuffling around him, and as he opened his eyes again he saw the ship’s crew start to emerge from the doors hinged to the deck. One had an eye patch, and another had scars up and down his arms. They were all filthy, heavily tanned, hideous, muscular and scowling at him.

"Look at what we got 'ere," a crewmember with very little neck taunted.

"*Fresh meat*," another answered with a sinister grin.

Caldwell swallowed audibly as the group of men began to edge closer.

He wondered if he would ever see England again.

***

London, England

The Earl and Countess of Stanton left the Bellington Ball early and as they made their departure, the ballroom erupted into applause and laughter. Smiling, Cy whisked his bride away. He was planning on locking himself and his wife in the bedroom for a full week, and then maybe he would let them out to rejoin the world.

His heart swelled when he escorted her into his townhouse. He would never have to be separated from her again. Her home was with him now, and he could not wait to have her in his bed, every night for the rest of their lives. The thought was both enjoyable and humbling.

When they were in the foyer, he scooped her up into his arms, causing her to laugh.

"What are you doing?" she asked, her face flushing beautifully.

"Taking you to bed. I thought it was obvious."

"Of course. You have also alerted all our servants to your intention."

He looked at her tenderly. "We are married, sweetheart. Let them speak of my love for you as well as my unquenchable desire."

"There are worse things for them to know, I suppose," she teased.

Carrying her up the stairs and down the hallway, he stopped in front of a closed door. "This is your room."

Grasping the knob with one hand, he stepped into the bedroom. He enjoyed watching her mouth part in awe when she saw the splendor of the room. It was decorated in pale pink and white and lit with a dozen candles.

"I had the room redone. Do you like it?"

"It is beautiful. Will you put me down now?" she asked.

"No," he said good-naturedly.

He went to the connecting door and pushed it open to reveal his own bedroom, adorned with dark wood furniture, and red linens that covered the massive bed. Candles were lit, gilding everything in romantic shadows. It was a room for passion.

Unceremoniously, he dropped her in the middle of his large, spacious bed. Her eyes tracked him, but she made no move to scramble away.

"I plan on doing a lot of things to you in this bed," he said with a heated look.

"Things I will like?" she asked breathlessly.

"No doubt."

"I was going to put on a lace nightgown," she murmured as he began to strip out of his formal attire. He threw his jacket carelessly on the ground. His cravat followed moments later.

"It would be destroyed in a matter of seconds." He reached for his trousers.

She sighed when he stood before her, unashamedly naked. His erection was hard, throbbing, and ready for her. Her green eyes glowed with desire.

"Do you realize, dear husband, that this is the first time we will have made love in a bed?"

He laughed, his voice thick with lust, when he said, "True. Our other trysts have involved rather uncomfortable settings."

"And yet you still gave me so much pleasure. I would like to do the same for you."

She got up off the bed and kneeled in front of him. She ran her hands up his muscular thighs and then slowly caressed him. Cy leaned his head back in exquisite bliss. She moved her hands to grasp behind his thighs and pulled his body closer to her waiting, greedy mouth. She presented an erotic picture, on her knees, still in her ball gown with her hair pinned back. When her tongue lightly touched the head of his shaft, he thought he was going to burst from her tender assault. She continued to lick and sucked gently, and Cy groaned.

"Your skin is so soft and hot to the touch," she whispered. "It is almost like you have a fever."

Cy thought he was going to die from the delectable torture, and so he took a step back and helped Ivy to her feet.

"Did you not like it? Did I do it wrong?"

He kissed her hard on the mouth and his tongue moved to touch hers. "You were perfect, and I loved every moment of it, but I want to feel your skin against mine. I need to take you into my arms and plunge into your heat. I must be inside you," he growled.

He removed the pins from her hair, pleased when it fell in gentle curls down her back. His hands went to her dress, but his rabid desire strained his patience as he tried to unbutton the tiny hindrances to her gown. Cursing, her ripped it, sending the tatters of the ruined dress to the floor.

"Oh, yes, I see what you mean. That could have been my nightgown," she murmured.

He went for her chemise and helped her out of it and then lay down on the bed on his back. When she looked confused, he held out his hand and said, "Come here, love, I will show you. Straddle me."

She did as commanded. His hard length teased the wet entrance to her body, and Cy's heart hammered in his chest.

Gently touching her thigh, his hand moved between her legs. She was slick and ready for him, and he could not wait any longer. He urged her body onto his and he grinned when Ivy gasped in enjoyment as he penetrated her. He went in deep. When he began to guide her hips to teach her the rhythm, she gave in. Cy bucked beneath her, loving the feel of his wife's creamy flesh in his hands as she rode him. Faster and faster they went, until she cried out her fulfillment. Cy thrust one last time and came with a shattering release.

She lay on his chest, and pressed her face to his shoulder. "Loving you will be the death of me," she whispered.

He chuckled and replied, “The night is far from over, love, and when my strength returns I will show you.”

“How long might that be?” she wondered.

Rolling her onto her back, he grinned. “Sooner than we both thought.”

***

It was early afternoon the next day when Ivy awoke. She snuggled into her husband’s arms, pressing a kiss to his bare chest. Their night of passion had been exhilarating and thoroughly exhausting, and she was famished.

Quietly, she got out of bed, went to her bedroom and pulled on a robe. She rang for a maid and requested a breakfast tray. Traipsing back into Cy’s room, she frowned when she saw he was still asleep. She climbed into bed and let her hand rove over his hot skin.

He stirred, but his eyes were still closed when he pushed her hand lower. She chuckled and obliged, caressing him gently for a few moments.

“What a pleasant way to wake up.” His voice was raspy with sleep and lust.

“I have a surprise for you.”

“So far I like it.”

“Not *that*,” she said with a laugh.

He finally opened his eyes and frowned. “You are dressed.”

“No, I am in a robe. I rang for a breakfast tray.”

Scratching his stubbly jaw, he sat up. There was a knock on the door and Ivy went to answer it. She took the tray from the maid and brought it back to bed. When they finished tea and pastries, she got up.

"Where are you going?" he demanded when he saw her walk to her own room.

"To get dressed."

"Why?"

"You are insatiable, My Lord," she purred.

"Ivy!"

"Get dressed, Cy. I want to show you something."

He did as she commanded, but grumbled when she insisted they leave the bedroom.

"We can come back up later," she promised with a smile. Taking his hand, she led him to the ballet studio, and removed her outer clothes.

"What are you doing?"

"Dancing for you," she said.

"In your chemise and a pair of breeches?"

"I told you it was a surprise."

She tied on her ballet slippers and then moved to the bar. She started her warm up and went to the center of the room. Taking a deep breath, she raised an elegant arm and began a series of movements that included twirls and pirouettes. She danced around the room, leaping like a graceful, long-legged animal. Time stopped for her as she shared the deepest part of herself with her husband. When she finished, she turned to look at him.

He was staring at her with raw passion.

"Cy?" she asked, as he stalked towards her. Gripping her by the arms, he kissed her soundly, his mouth slanting over hers.

"You are sight to behold when you dance," he said between kisses. Backing her up against one of the mirrors, he spun her around, their eyes colliding in the glass.

She was breathing hard when Cy's hand stroked her breast and pinched a nipple through her chemise. His fingers tickled their way down her body, playing with the juncture at her thighs over her breeches.

Untying the string that held them up, he let them fall and pool at her feet. She stepped out of them, and he rubbed his erection against her back. His fingers sought her again, as the reflection of their eyes clashed.

Their breathing was labored as he fumbled with his trouser buttons with his free hand. His shaft sprang free and he groaned. When he removed his fingers from inside of her, they were glistening with her honey. Taking his length into his hand, he eased into her, filling her. Gasping, she leaned into him, her eyes never leaving his as he pumped into her from behind.

"You are beautiful," he gritted. "Stunning, desirous." He slammed into her and she sobbed in relief as her release claimed her. With a shout, he followed.

"Did you ever expect this to happen when you built this studio for me?" she asked, when she could finally manage a coherent thought.

Lifting his head from her shoulder, he stared into the mirror, meeting her eyes. "No."

"Do you think it will happen again?" she asked hopefully.

He laughed. "Absolutely."

***

"Sophia has a dress fitting tomorrow morning and then in the afternoon we are attending Lady Essex's musicale," Lady Baker said to her husband as they ambled through Hyde Park.

"Hmm," Lord Baker replied absently.

"Are you listening to me?" Lady Baker demanded.

"Of course. You mentioned a musicale."

Momentarily appeased, she asked, "Would you like to join us?"

"Is Sophia singing?"

"Yes."

"Then absolutely not," Lord Baker said.

"You are horrible!" his wife cried. "Do you not love your daughter?"

Lord Baker raised bushy eyebrows. "Of course I love Sophia, but that does not make me deaf. She cannot sing."

"Lord Seaton praised her voice," Lady Baker said.

"Lord Seaton wants to marry our daughter. He would say anything!"

Stifling her laughter, Lady Baker playfully smacked her husband on the arm. "Sophia is quite fond of him."

"She is much too young to be thinking of marriage," Lord Baker harrumphed.

"Sophia is seventeen, My Lord."

"Much too young," he grumbled.

"Oh, my dear, you *do* love our daughter!" she tinkled.

"I said as much, did I not?"

They rounded the bend, assaulted by peals of laughter and good-natured shouting.

"What do you suppose?" Lady Baker asked, tugging her husband along, eager to discover the source. "Oh my."

Arriving in a small clearing by the lake, Lord and Lady Baker stopped abruptly. The Earl and Countess of Stanton were standing on the bank, each with a fishing pole in hand. The Countess of Stanton's dress hem was muddy, and her molten curls were cascading freely down her back.

"You are going to lose, My Lord," the Countess said, tossing an irreverent smile at her husband.

"I have been fishing for many more years than you," he rejoined.

The Countess snorted with laughter. "I have the raw talent, sir. I have caught three fish already, and we have only been here an hour. How many have you caught?"

"Slow and steady wins the race, my dear," the Earl said, gazing fondly at his new bride.

Lord Baker cleared his throat.

Turning her head, the Countess flushed. "Oh! Good afternoon, Lord Baker, Lady Baker.

"Good afternoon," Lord Baker murmured.

"You will have to excuse Stanton's inattention. He cannot fish and converse at the same time!"

Stanton grunted and then shouted with triumph, "I have caught one!"

Lady Baker gasped when Stanton drew his pole back and a glistening little fish flopped on the end of the line. The Countess set down her own pole and rushed to her husband's side, grasped the line and neatly disengaged the hook from the fish's mouth.

Tightening her grip on her husband's arm, Lady Baker nearly had an apoplectic fit.

After the Countess strung the dying fish on a string accommodating three others and settling it back into the lake, she said, "We have a wager you, you see. Stanton believes he is the better fisherman."

"I am, my dear, I am," Stanton groused.

"You fish?" Lord Baker inquired of the Countess.

"You wager?" Lady Baker queried.

"Yes," the Countess answered blithely.

"If you will excuse us, we need to concentrate on the matter at hand. There is much at stake here. Good day," Stanton said.

Duly dismissed, Lord and Lady Baker continued on their leisurely stroll. "They are quite eccentric," Lord Baker said finally.

"They are," his wife agreed.

"Who do you suppose will catch more fish?"

"Care to make a wager?" His wife sent him a sidewise glance and a smile.

Lord Baker grinned. "My money is on the Countess."

There was a shout from behind them. "Two!" came the Earl of Stanton's voice.

"I will take that bet, My Lord. If I win you must attend the musicale and paste a smile on your face and applaud our daughter's skill."

Lord Baker grimaced. “If I win, Sophia does not get engaged until next season.”

In a quick show of affection, Lady Baker reached up to kiss her husband’s cheek. “You have a bet, My Lord.”

Epilogue

Hampshire, England, One Year Later

Cy watched Ivy from the doorway of her ballet studio. Her movements were long and flowing, and he marveled at her strength as she did countless strengthening and conditioning exercises without becoming winded. He felt a surge of tenderness and desire mingle.

The first time she had danced for him was never far from his thoughts. Her skill and talent had overwhelmed him, and he had been unable to tear his eyes away from her. He wondered what would have happened if she had remained in Paris and become a prima ballerina. She would have had the world at her feet, no doubt.

He was glad she had settled for him.

"Good afternoon," Ivy said, twirling towards him and pressing a kiss to his lips.

"Good afternoon," Cy replied as he swept a hand down her dainty backside. "How are you feeling?"

"Sluggish and fat," she joked. "I cannot believe I have another three months before the baby comes. Soon, I will be too large to dance."

He placed a hand on her rounded belly. "You are beautiful, and you are carrying my child within you."

Ivy caressed his jaw with her delicate hand. "I could not imagine what my life would be like if I had never left Paris."

He gave her a lopsided smile. “I was wondering that, too. Though I am glad I took you to Paris after your sister’s wedding. I wanted to see where you grew up and practiced ballet.”

“I was glad to share my past with you.”

“I have some interesting news,” Cy said mysteriously.

“Oh? Do share.”

“I have received a missive from Lord Fitzgerald. His daughter is engaged.”

Ivy frowned. “I do not like hearing about the woman who caused us so much trouble.”

Cy looked at his wife and smiled. “Her interference only made us closer. I cannot help but want to thank her for that.”

Inclining her head in agreement, Ivy asked, “She is engaged, you say?”

“Yes, to a French count three times her age. Lord Fitzgerald also informed me that his daughter will be moving to France at the end of the month to be with her fiancé.”

Ivy grinned impishly. “I am *truly* sorry she will be unleashed among the unsuspecting people of Paris.” Her eyes twinkled mischievously as she went on, “But perhaps I should send her a gift.”

“A wedding present?” Cy asked as he touched Ivy’s glowing face.

“More like a thank you gift for moving far away from us.”

Cy threw back his head, shouted with laughter and then leaned over to kiss her lips.

“Any news on Lord Caldwell?” Ivy asked.

“None.”

"Perhaps he has turned pirate," she teased.

"Or found his dastardly end, but I suppose that would be too much to hope for. Can we not turn our attention to a happier topic? When are the guests arriving?" They were celebrating the Duchess's birthday, and though it was to be a small affair with only close friends and family, it would be quite extravagant.

"Grandmother is arriving this evening with Westonshire," Ivy said as Cy led her out of the studio and into the library. He sat her down in a comfortable leather chair so she could rest and took a seat next to her.

"Has she agreed to marry him yet?"

The aging Marquess had proposed to the Duchess a handful of times already, but the woman kept fending him off by saying she enjoyed her freedom and independence.

"Not yet, but she will," Ivy predicted.

"Perhaps instead of marriage, they will come to a different arrangement."

"What ever do you mean?"

He raised his eyebrows. "They could become lovers."

"At their age!" Ivy sputtered. "Surely, you jest."

"Your Grandmother is a duchess, she can do anything she wants," Cy joked. "How old is she turning?"

"She would not say. Apparently, even a duchess ages."

"And your sister, when are she and Bedford arriving?"

"In a few days. Bedford is being overly protective due to her delicate condition. He does not want her to travel, but she insists. I am so glad our firstborns will be close in age."

"It is good fortune," Cy agreed. "Your brother, Robert? When is he due to arrive?"

Six months after Cy and Ivy had been married, Robert, the Duke of Cavehill, had finally returned from his trek across the continent. Though initially reserved around Ivy and Willow, he quickly became a doting older brother.

"Tomorrow sometime. I wish there was some lovely young woman I could throw in his direction. It is time he married."

"You sound like your grandmother," Cy ribbed. "It seems you have her matchmaking tendencies."

"I just want him as happy as we are," she said with a grin. "Lady Sophia is a lovely young woman."

"The Lady Sophia Baker?" Cy inquired. "Oh, the Devil take it! You will not enlist me in your plot. When are the Langleys coming?"

"They will be here tomorrow morning with their two children. We will have a brood here for weeks!"

Cy chuckled and patted his wife's belly. "This is the start of our very own brood."

"Do you wish for a boy or a girl? Silly question. You would like a boy to carry on the title."

"Eventually," Cy agreed, "but I hope our first is a girl."

"You do?"

"Yes. I want her to be just like her mother." His voice was tender.

"In what ways?" she asked.

"I hope she has your hair." His hand reached to touch her silken tresses. "Your eyes." He placed a kiss on each of her eyelids. "Your heart, and your skill with ballet."

"You want your daughter to learn to dance? It would be considered quite improper."

Cy smiled. "Also very much like her mother, no?"

"Oh, Cy," she whispered, her eyes tearing. "I love you." She attempted to move into his arms, but her bulk made it awkward and they both laughed. "This brood of ours…how many will it entail?"

"I was hoping for five," he answered.

"Five? You will have to remain very attentive to my *needs*, My Lord, if you expect such a large family," she warned with a lustful laugh.

"Do you think I am not up for the challenge? Do you dare question my virility?" he gasped in mock outrage.

Her gaze drifted to her stomach. "I do not think there is any doubt about your virility," Ivy said. "If you can contend with my tears and emotional outbursts, my odd desire for strange food in the middle of the night, then I suppose I can give you five children."

"A good number to strive for. It will keep us occupied."

She arched a brow. "As if you needed a reason to remain locked in our bedroom."

He grinned. "Before our house is overrun with friends and family, we better make use of our privacy." He stretched out his hand to help her up.

Taking it, she rose slowly. Tugging it free, her hands went to her clothes.

"What are you doing?" he asked.

"The library will suffice for the moment."

Smiling wickedly, Cy locked the library door and reached for his shirt. "With your appetites, my dear, I cannot help but think five children is a paltry number."

Her chemise hit the floor. "At the moment, I am ravenous for you."

Cy dropped to his knees in front of her, resting his hands on her firm derriere and pulled her towards him. "So gluttonous," he murmured. "Let me see if I can slake your need."

His tongue touched her and she threw her head back in abandon, her fingers gripping his hair. "Not in this lifetime, my love, not in this life time."

End

Thank you so much for reading! Please consider leaving a review! Reviews help authors find new readers!

About the author:

Samantha Garman lives and writes in Brooklyn, NY. She enjoys single malt Scotch, cheese and fluffy dogs.

Connect with Samantha Garman online:
Twitter: @samgarman
Facebook: Samantha Garman-Author

Stay in the loop about new releases by visiting Samantha Garman's Amazon Page and subscribing!

15325873R00143

Printed in Great Britain
by Amazon